The Loan Shark of Gangnam District

Onyeka Nwelue, born in 1988, is a Nigerian scholar,filmmaker, jazz musician and publisher, who has published over 30 books, the most popular being the Crime Fiction Lovers' Awards-winning *The Strangers of Braamfontein*, described by Nobel Laureate, Wole Soyinka, as 'raunchy.' Nwelue was an Academic Visitor to the University of Oxford and Visiting Scholar in the University of Cambridge. He was a Visiting Research Fellow at Ohio University and a Research Associate at the University of Johannesburg. His documentary *The House of Nwapa* was nominated in the Best Documentary category at the 2017 Africa Movie Academy Awards. The next year, Nwelue adapted his novella *Island of Happiness* into an Igbo film, Agwaetiti Obiụtọ, which was nominated in the Best First Feature Film and Best Film in an African Language categories at the 2018 Africa Movie Academy Awards and won the Best Film by a Director at the Newark International Film Festival.

In 2024, his biopic of Emeka Ojukwu, *Other Side of History*, was screened at the Toronto International Film Festival.

Nwelue is the director of Africa Center Mexico.

The Loan Shark of Gangnam District

Onyeka Nwelue

Abibiman
Publishing

New York & London

First published in the United Kingdom in 2025
by Abibiman Publishing
www.abibimanpublishing.com

Copyright © 2025 Onyeka Nwelue

ISBN: 978-1-0685027-8-1

Cover design by Fred Martins

Printed at Clays UK

The Women of Biafra Review

The story of Biafra...that should never be forgotten
- Frederick Forsyth

Nwelue doesn't shy away from the brutal realities of war. The Biafran War novel has become an established genre within Nigerian literature and known for stories that skillfully depict the visceral sense of war.
- Brittlepaper Review

The Women of Biafra is a short but highly effective novel. Using plain, straightforward language – peppered with some brilliantly evocative similes – Nwelue vividly portrays the atrocities committed against Biafran civilians by Nigerian troops, and one woman's dogged determination to survive for the sake of her loved ones.
- Dr. Alice Violett

The Women of Biafra is a captivating and evocative work of fiction set against the tumultuous backdrop of the Nigerian Civil War
- The Secret Book Review UK

Onyeka Nwelue's *The Women of Biafra* is a harrowing exploration of the Nigerian Civil War through the eyes of those often overlooked: women. Structured in a dramatic, episodic format, the novel plunges readers into the visceral horrors of conflict, offering a stark and unflinching portrayal of human suffering.

Nwelue's mastery lies in his ability to evoke raw emotion. The closing scene of Part II, "Enemy Territory," is a case in point. The graphic depiction of Mark's mutilated body and Mama Idu's heart-wrenching grief is both shocking and profoundly moving. It sets the tone for a narrative that spares no detail in its exploration of war's brutal realities.
- The BagusNG Review

I am pleased that the author took on the challenge of putting this pain into words bevaise the story of their plight needed to be told, to be shared, so that people could learn from such ways.

I was so hooked on this booked.

- Bwignall

The Nigerian Mafia: Mumbai Review

The Nigerian Mafia Mumbai by Onyeka Nwelue is a phenomenal book in many regards. It has culture, crime, cult, and lust, all packaged in a unique, original voice of Onyeka Nwelue. It'll make you laugh and smile, until everything fades away in the end.

- Bombayreads

Onyeka Nwelue has been a world traveler with long experience in both Lagos and Mumbai. I am deeply impressed with how the author uses the stream of consciousness memoir to impress upon readers just how thoroughly corrupt and yet still somewhat sympathetic Mbadiegwu is.

- Scintilla Book Review

I really should read more novels by African authors, this one by prollific Nigerian author Nwelue was only the second I've read this year.

I wasn't entirely sure what to expect of a novel that is titled *Nigerian Mafia: Mumbai* with mentions of Nollywood and Bollywood, the end of the blurb stresses the former concerns rather than the latter: 'The Nigerian Mafia is a tale of violence, drugs, human trafficking, murder and sex.'

- Anna Bookbel Review

The Nigerian Mafia Mumbai, by Onyeka Nwelue, presents a raw and unflinching account of the lives and experiences of African migrants in Mumbai and other parts of India. Uche's narration is stark, unforgiving, and brutal, offering a compelling insight into their struggles.

–Suleiman Ahmed is the author of Trouble in Valhalla

The Nigerian Mafia: Johannesburg Review

The Nigerian Mafia: Johannesburg is a blistering run through a morally corrupt yet interesting man's attempt to find a new life in a new country. An interesting, if extremely short, read.

- Mail and Guardian Magazine South Africa

In this very brief episode in the life of Uche - a Nigerian hitman - we are guided through his misadventures in the City of Gold (Johannesburg). After escaping Sao Paulo, Uche finds himself in Jozi where his day-job as a hired killer leads him to run-ins with loan sharks, organised Chinese crime syndicates in Bruma, and the general chaos of life in Yeoville. After a drug-deal gone wrong, Uche flees once again to Cape Town to find peace. While he is temporarily able to achieve this once he meets Kanya - a beautiful, wise young woman who he quickly falls for, the utopia is only fleeting as his life slowly begins to fall into disarray once again.

While the subject matter tackled in this novella is captivating and eye-opening, the story is lacking in focus, and proper character exploration. Uche is a man on the run, unable to settle because of his choice (arguable perhaps) to pursue a life of crime. We see, in him, the quest to settle down and lead a normal life but the underworld of the Nigerian Mafia seems to keep pulling him back whenever he attempts to. Aside from this, the reader is not offered anything deeper as far as understanding Uche's motives. This, to a strong degree, sterilises the story. This insufficient character development also makes the story appear rather rushed and incomplete.

Reading this as a written account of crime syndicates in South Africa will probably increase one's satisfaction with the book. As a novella, due to the superficial way in which the author handles the presentation of characters - including the MP - it falls drastically short of being the truly captivating short read it could be had the author spent more time on it.

- Thabs, Review Goodreads

Strangers of Braamfontein Review

"*The Strangers of Braamfontein* is a perceptive and vigorous tale of people trapped in dire circumstances"

- *Kirkus Reviews.*

'*The Strangers of Braamfontein*' is heavily peopled with characters as dark as the night who are cohabiting in a brutal place where death is cheap. Raw, gritty, fast-paced, this is not a book you can glance through because it will force you to keep turning the pages. It will make you shiver with trepidation. It is such a searing read. This is a book to love.

- *Olukorede S. Yishau, The Lagos Review.*

"*The Strangers of Braamfontein* is one of those crime novels that hits you in the gut and before you can recover another powerful blow is delivered. It's a story of corruption, gangland violence, sex trafficking, modern slavery and murder. All of this is seen from the perspective of the people brutalised, abused and discarded and those profiting and perpetuating their misery."

- *Paul Burke, Crime Fiction Lover.*

"The novel features a colorful and sprawling cast of characters, each motivated by the dictates of a world where survival is in deed for the fittest."

- *ALESIA ALEXANDER, Brittle Paper.*

"There is no downtime with *The Strangers of Braamfontein*. The pacing is fast and is sustained all through to the last page. I like the character Osas, mostly. He represents the hopeful African youth who travels to break out of the dire situation at home. The drug lord Papi is another character I find very interesting, and then there is the prostitute who falls in love with Osas. This is my second time reading the book and I don't trust myself well enough to not come back to it repeatedly."

- *Ikenna Okeh, Author of The Operative.*

"Onyeka Nwelue's *The Strangers of Braamfontein* is timely and urgent, a necessary read, in view of recent happenings in South Africa. Moreover, it is a novel that African migration and diaspora scholars may find relevant in discussing intra-continental migration and its complexities—insofar as they have the appetite for its grisly servings."

- Uche Umezurike, Author of Double wahala,
Double trouble.

"*The Strangers of Braamfontein* is a portrait of broken dreams. It is a book of piranhas destined for a fatal ending."

- Miterrand Okorie, Nigerian Abroad.

"Funny, lively and compelling characters, Onyeka Nwelue's *The Strangers of Braamfontein* is a memorable read. "

–Jumoke Verissimo, author of A Small Silence

"*The Strangers Of Braamfontein* holds up a cracked, blood-stained mirror to modern, post-colonial Africa. Tackling themes of xenophobia, homophobia, racism, sex trafficking and more, *The Strangers Of Braamfontein* lays bare the desperate lengths people will go to in search of a better life.

- Megan Thomas, Buzz Mag.

"*The Strangers of Braamfontein* is a grim, grisly view of post-Apartheid South Africa, and among its wide range of characters there are barely any who aren't morally compromised. But, for all its bleakness, it sizzles with a visceral, pulpy energy."

- Alastair Mabbott, The Herald of Scotland.

"If you want a different book, with a spotlight on a world a long way from your own back door, this is well worth a try and will linger in the memory. You can't help but keep your fingers crossed that for some, there is hope and a glimmer of light."

- Adrian Magson,
The author 23 Spy and Crime Thrillers.

Onyeka's style of writing is straightforward. *The Strangers of Braamfontein* educates you, entertains you and throws harsh realities at your face. The novel portrays a typical 21st century African millennial society that exposes the tyranny of government officials and leaders. It will hook you to the end and keep you hanging on a cliff. No crime fiction comes close to this. This is simply the best I have read in a very long time.

- Chidimma Eze.

The Strangers of Braamfontein is a thriller. The very best of them you could possibly find out there. It is realistic and it shocks you to your roots, making you question the things you think you know. The characters are relatable. This is a strong and deeply felt novel. I enjoyed it. I am impressed and hooked and I am sure that many others will say the same of this book.

- Daniella Eze.

The Strangers of Braamfontein is a well written book and the plot tells of the depth of the writer's understanding of the human condition in many African mega cities. This is a story with twists and turns that you can never predict. It keeps your heart pacing and you don't realize when you begin to take responsibility for the characters. Onyeka really gets me hooked on this one, and he has to keep this up. I can't wait for his next crime novel.

-Nwodo Henry.

Onyeka Nwelue sets a quick pace in *"The Strangers Of Braamfontein"* as he masterfully narrates the harsh realities that plays out in Braamfontein. This story is set against the backdrop of organized crime in its undiluted forms. The Strangers of Braamfontein is so good. It is a masterpiece and I admit that I have read it more than once.

- *Chukwunyere Ejike.*

I have never read anything like this written by an African. *The Strangers of Braamfontein* is a great crime tale. I will be glad if many young people read this novel. It will open their eyes to the reality of what life could possibly turn out for an immigrant in a foreign land.

- *Francis Ifeanyichukwu Okwara.*

No Crime Novel Comes Close To The Strangers of Braamfontein

Onyeka Nwelue knows what is at stake and he does so well with *The Strangers of Braamfontein* in portraying a 21st century Africa doomed by the sting of corruption, crime and desperation. This novel puts the spotlight on the ugly influence of intimidation, mismanagement of power by government officials and the leaders. especially their complicity in the rate at which crime and illegality attracts young people who hold onto the "get rich quick" syndrome.

Quite remarkable is the writer's figurative attempt to depict the life of drug dealing in all of its grandeur and danger, leading us on with his engaging narrative through scenes after scenes of violence, sex and betrayal.

I like his style of writing. It is straightforward. It makes you take a dive in from the first pages and excites you from the onset and all through the entire pages of the book, educating you, entertaining you and throwing harsh realities at your face. Onyeka invested well enough in vibrant characters depicting them as passionate and real. It is with this same real passion that Onyeka have written and presented this book. It will hook you to the end and keep you hanging on a cliff. No crime fiction comes close to this. This is simply the best I have read in a very long time.

-Chidimma Eze.

This Is Onyeka's Perfect Outing As a Writer

The strangers of Braamfontein is a thriller, the very best of them you could possibly find out there. It is realistic and it shocks you to your roots, making you question the things you think you know. The action takes your breath away; you always want to know what happens next to your favourite character. It is the social and moral oddity that captures me about this book and Onyeka did a really great job in highlighting these things in ways that gets the plot going forward. Ingenious.

The characters are relatable. I mean if you have ever had an experience with the rough side of things in Africa, you will easily relate with the characters and the worlds in which they find themselves. I like it that Onyeka entertains us within surroundings that we can identify. Prostitution, drugs, human trafficking have done so much damage to societies in Africa and this is the main focus of the book. We also see it in the book that the governments of affected societies are doing nothing to stop these things. I find this to be honest and courageous of the writer and such values ought to be recognized.

The world that the writer painted in this book is a harsh one. In it, only the strongest survive. It is a jungle. A place where A world recognized for its greed, violence, betrayal, lust and ruthless use of power. Yet it is the reality that we should be strong enough to confront. It is the world of millions of people, their reality.

This is a strong and deeply felt novel. I enjoyed it. I am impressed and hooked and I am sure that many others will say the same of this book.

- Daniella Eze.

Nwelue's Breakthrough As a Writer
Is This Crime Novel

The Strangers of Braamfontein is a well written book and the plot tells of the depth of the writer's understanding of the human condition in many African mega cities. His depiction of Braamfontein is no different from the realities of many others in Nairobi or Lagos or any other major African metropolitan cities where poverty is and desperation stares you in the face. Onyeka Nwelue must be a master of suspense to have achieved what he did with this book. I began reading it and it swept me off. There is hardly anything about it that isn't familiar to an observant eye. It mirrors the human condition, a testament to how easily our humanity can be eroded when we dwell for too long with hunger and desperation.

I am drawn to the character, Osas. He had left Nigeria with the hope of making it big n South Africa. But to his surprise he had exchanged one desperate level for another. Life in South Africa takes him through a story of betrayal, love, lust, and fear, all of which beams and wanes at every turn of Osas' life and with the interaction he has with every other characters. Oh, and as for other characters, they are as indepth as Osas. I don't exactly like thinking about the Chamai character. He breaks my heart. I wish things have ended up differently for him with the closeted homosexual Chike. Btu instead, Chike takes advantage of his desperation and things ended up with Chamai the way it did. Really breaks my heart.

This is a story with twists and turns that you can never predict. It keeps your heart pacing and you don't realize when you begin to take responsibility for the characters. Onyeka really gets me hooked on this one, and he has to keep this up. I can't wait for his next crime novel.

- Nwodo Henry.

The Strangers of Braamfontein Is So Good

From the very beginning, Onyeka Nwelue sets a quick pace in *"The Strangers Of Braamfontein"* as he masterfully narrates the harsh realities that plays out in Braamfontein. This story is set against the backdrop of organized crime in its undiluted forms. I noticed my eyes were wet and my heart beat faster than usual as I read Ruth narrating her story to her girls, yes her girls.

I don't know why I am more drawn to the character of Ruth and her girls. Every time, there are stories of girls trafficked out of African countries by prostitution rings, sometimes unwillingly and sometimes willingly. This is one book that treats the situation in a way that entertains, questions and enlightens the reader. I am sure it should be a reference point whenever issues of trafficking and organized crime is being discussed.

I had imagined a turn of events when I got to that point where the prostitute, April, gets pregnant for Osas, the drug dealer, who also has a secret thing going with April's boss, Ruth. But then it had turned out differently and I had been left wondering how sleek Onyeka Nwelue is with spinning his plot in such a way that made a fool of me in trying to be predictive. The Strangers of Braamfontein is so good. It is a masterpiece and I admit that I have read it more than once.

- Chukwunyere Ejike.

The Strangers of Braamfontein
Is a Great Crime Tale

My favorite character is the young Nigerian, Osas, who travels to Braamfontein so as to make it big. His story is an honest depiction of the fate of millions of Nigerians and Africans who travel overseas in the hope of better lives and success. Most times they don't relate their experiences and we don't know what life for them abroad is. But with *The Strangers of Braamfontein*, we can see realities play before our eyes and we can enjoy these realities as the entertainment that they are.

I have never read anything like this written by an African. It takes a certain level of boldness to write about issues like this in such a detailed manner. Maybe this is what writing should be, and if we can look at our world as closely as Onyeka Nwelue is making us do with this book, then we can begin to have honest conversations that are channeled towards making better societies for ourselves.

The character, Papi, is another one I like. He is a clear example of what happens when we become too comfortable in predatory worlds. The jungle is what it is, and even predators could be preyed upon. I like the fact that Nwelue portrays that if ever a place have a reputation for crime, it is so because people in high places who are supposed to protect the interests of the people who elected them there are beneficiaries of the institutionalized rot. We see this with the policemen who are on the payroll of Papi. I love what Nwelue did with this. I am impressed.

I will be glad if many young people read this novel. It will open their eyes to the reality of what life could possibly turn out for an immigrant in a foreign land.

- Francis Ifeanyichukwu Okwara.

"...Like a persistent itch that only goes away by scratching, it is hard to ignore this writer."

- Eromo Egbejule, The Guardian (UK)

"The literary world can do with more babies from the bassinet of "The Strangers of Braamfontein"!"

- Wole Soyinka, Nobel Laureate.

Praise for Burnt

"Spiders, snakes, disco, paternal violence, Jacques Brel, literary Lagos, Africans in Europe - it's a breathless series of vignettes, anecdotes and narratives we meet in Onyeka Nwelue's Burnt, the whole related fast in rapidly successive moments. The voice is direct, talking you through events. Sometimes it assumes the personal, sometimes it shifts through the overheard and imagined. It is very much a multi-cultural world, the book itself a city of sorts where every window is open. So you keep watching and listening."

- George Szirtes, author of The Slant Door (1979)

"Onyeka Nwelue has written himself. These poems are vintage Onyeka: raw, honest and beautiful. Always edgy."

- Bwesigye bwa Mwesigir, author of Fables Out of Nyanja

"Daringly different and unarguably exquisite, these poems posses unseen but felt arm that leads your entire being through boulevards decorated with brilliant narratives that keep you walking without stopping, but yearning for more. Here is a delectable oeuvre that resonates. One more feather on OnyekaNwelue's baronial hat. Yes."

- Echezonachukwu Nduka, author of Echoes of Sentiments

"Sublime, strange and experimental. I read Burnt with a great admiration for Onyeka Nwelue. Each flow, each sentence, each line has something tasteless about it, yet is bewitching."

- Chika Onyenezi, author of Sea Lavender

For my friends

Omojola Ayodele Gabriel

Stanley Amos

Promise Ovuike

&

Hyung Jae

이형재

Nneka Nnanna

Thank you all.

Contents

Prologue

Jin-ho sat on the edge of the bed in his daughter's Westwood Village home, thinking about the long flight from Los Angeles to Seoul on Korean Air, as Soo-ah packed his bags into the black trolley. They were surrounded by the soft glow of Westwood's Mediterranean-style design. The Spanish-tile roofs, flowered courtyards, echoed of UCLA's academic calm in every pane and paseo.

Outside, Koreatown stirred with life. Nearly 230,000 Koreans lived in the Los Angeles area, making it the largest Korean community outside the peninsula. Its neon signs, BBQ joints, language academies, and Asiana Airlines offices pulsed with homeland energy in an American city.

Soo-ah calmly folded Jin-ho's shirts. She'd finished her master's in architecture at UCLA and had participated in designing a pavilion near Wilshire Boulevard in Koreatown—a space blending California light with Hanok curves. She'd also begun teaching part-time, nurturing future architects amid Glaswegian skylines.

Soo-ah spoke softly. "Here." She zipped the trolley shut. "Do you have your passport and phone charger?"

Jin-ho nodded, finger brushing the trolley's handle. "Yes. Thank you."

The accent was silky smooth. As Soo-ah spoke, her consonants clipped, her vowels carrying the subtle rise and fall of Gyeonggi dialect, the prestige dialect of Seoul and the national standard. Jin-ho felt an upsurge of joy that nearly lifted him from his chair.

Years in Los Angeles hadn't diluted her voice. Instead, she had blended her identity into her English with dexterity, her Korean heritage perfectly wrapped in fluent American cadence.

"Appa, don't forget your wristwatch," she said.

Even after a decade teaching architecture at UCLA and co-designing community spaces in Koreatown, her inflection remained unmistakably hers. She said "Appa" with a fond nostalgia. When she laughed, the soft hum of her breathy giggle threaded through. The shifting between tongues felt seamless but meaningful; she hadn't needed to sacrifice her mother tongue, even in America. When she asked if he wanted tea, he smiled at the comfort in her phrasing.

Jin-ho's chest tightened with pride. He remembered teaching her Korean syllables on thetatami mats when she was small, tracing strokes of vowels with trembling fingers. He'd worried she'd lose all that education in the pursuit of her dreams abroad, as she took up teaching career in UCLA and design studios. But it was intact. Untouched. In her pitch, in her cadence, in shy shifts between Korean form and English completion.

As his fingers gripped the trolley handle, he was suffused with warmth and delight that his daughter hadn't shed her identity. Her voice still carried the strands of both Los Angeles and Seoul, a blend of identity. An identity marked by resilience, especially in the way she honoured her cultural heritage. In every polite particle and hardened consonant, he heard her mother's, Min-seo's, lessons about honorifics, family deference, those anecdotes passed on over kitchen tables. He heard the moral code he'd hoped would survive them both.

He looked up. Soo-ah paused, glancing at him. She smiled, then asked in English, "Dad, are you ready to go?"

He rose, his voice heavy but steady. "Yes."

She paused at the door, exchanging a quiet look with him, a small smile starting on her lips.

"Dad, I'll miss you."

He forced a smile back at her, fear clutching his chest.

"I'll be back soon. Seoul will feel the same, only with new pain."

"I know. But I will still miss you." She dove into his arms, wrapping herself in an embrace.

They stepped out into the afternoon warmth. The neighbourhood smelled of grilled kimchi tacos and cold brew. Westwood's familiar hum of cafes like Mary & Robbs and Lavender Bistro intertwined with local students rushing past for Hammer Museum events or Geffen Playhouse shows.

Soo-ah started the car, backing out past brocade cobblestones. Jin-ho looked out the window: students in backpacks, old and young, people whose Identities had been mixed, like his daughter's.

They drove straight to LAX Terminal 2. Lights on Wilshire blurred past. In the parking station, they sat in the car for a while, allowing the silence wash over them. Then Jin-ho said, "You've done so much in LA, built bridges between cultures."

Soo-ah replied tenderly, "I stand on what you built, Dad."

Finally, they got out of the car and made for the terminal. Soo-ah carried the trolley forward, pausing in the flowing sea of passengers.

"Call me when you land," she said amidst the hum of voices.

Jin-ho nodded solemnly.

"Always. Please."

They embraced, her arms small around his frail frame. Then she stepped away, turning with one last look before disappearing into the crowd. Jin-ho took the trolley and wheeled it towards the Korean Air sign. He let out a controlled and deliberate breath.

And then he walked forward, a journey bound by love and haunted by shadows.

Most people can't start things or most people can't finish things, but if you can start something and finish something, you're going to be fine.

— MIN JIN LEE

Book
ONE

Chapter 1

Shadows in the Bar

The neon glow of Seolleung-ro shimmered in layers of modern ambition and hidden textures. Sidewalks pulsed with foot traffic from Seolleung Station, office crowds spilling out like rivers of suits.

At 409 Teheran-ro, the Starbucks Reserve branch catered to tech workers and mid-ranking executives. Its glass façade gleamed, and the aroma of grapefruit honey black tea wafted through open doors. About a block over, the Ronnefeldt Tea House hummed with its legendary services, tea leaves steeping in fine porcelain, calm and deliberate in its aesthetic.

A few meters down Seolleung-ro 93-gil, the dependable A Twosome Place café extended tables under a white umbrella and soft lighting, drawing office workers in for Americano and café latte breaks amid quiet chatter. Beside it, Super Coffee – Seolleungro presented seasonal strawberry milk and oversized iced drinks. Further on, Sweet EPI served up desserts of madeleines, coffee jelly, and delicate cakes, its cosy, pastel-hued interior even more inviting.

Yet, just fifty paces to the side, in a narrow alley branching off Teheran-ro, the mood shifted. The corporate sheen dissolved into flickering plastic tarpaulin tents and the hiss of cooking oil. Here, pojangmacha stalls spilled onto the pavement: tteokbokki lava-red and bubbling, odeng skewers sliding into hot broth, dakkochi brushed with honey-garlic sauce and sesame seeds. The air was intoxicating, smoky, oily, alive.

One stand, a battered cart, was run by Dae-jung, where he sold honey-glazed hotteok and steaming gyeranppang. Skewers sizzled over flames. Steam curled into the neon haze. The vendor offered grudging smiles to strangers lost in the street's half-darkness. Occasional gangly office-workers from nearby towers stopped by, poring over spicy broth before disappearing into the glass-facade highways above.

Beyond the veneer of commerce and the mix of aroma and heat, Seolleung-ro had the glints of politics and power charging in the tall buildings. Rumours among the locals had it that the stretch of buildings housing firms like Samsung and Kakao, offered more than employment. Stories had it that real estate deals, political favours, off-the-books funding happened in those buildings.

But these were more than tales. The former mayor, Lee Jae-myung, had been indicted over development corruption in Seongnam. Prosecutors alleged he colluded with private developers, appropriating municipal projects in exchange for bribes. Lobbyists got five-year sentences, and political fallout continued. And yet the buildings stayed tall, the suits kept signing deals. No arrests of the big names. No penalties that topple the firms. The residents of Gangnam were worse off, as they were on preserving property value and supporting whoever protected their investments, allowing political immunity to run deep.

Those towers waded off justice with ease, enlisting the police in their corruption. Samsung and Kakao office blocks on Seolleung-ro watched over the gritty scene, a daily reminder that wealth, law, and politics decided who remained visible and who stayed hidden.

Jin-ho's Risky Bar stood amidst this chaos of ambition and power. With its battered door and a red bulb, it was tucked beneath a karaoke bar and next to a small tailor shop (a nod to Chong Ro Tailor's legacy nearby). Inside, Jin-ho stood, leaning behind his counter, tracing distant café chatter and the sizzling of street food with equal awareness. The dual worlds of café comfort and alleyway grit existed side by side, just like his life, trapped between ambition and survival. It was the usual thing in Seolleung-ro, a place where the sizzle of street food met the sheen of hidden cafés. A meeting point of resources and despair.

Inside the bar, the air tasted of spilled soju and stale cigarette ash. Jin-ho's hands moved on autopilot: wiping a mahogany counter, stacking soju bottles, pouring barley tea. He glanced at the entrance, expecting to see Soo-ah.

"Appa!"

Her voice floated in suddenly, hushed and loving. She held up her sketchbook to her chest, eyes bright. "Look, it's a new design for my school project."

He offered her a kindly smile, obviously exhausted. Yet, he couldn't hide the pride in his eyes. "You've been practicing again. It looks amazing." Jin-ho poured her some juice into a small glass.

"Daddy…" she hesitated, flipping the page. "I want to try some fashion illustration, full time."

"What about architectural designs?"

"It's all the same. I can do many things at the same time." A smiled was planted on her lips.

He paused. "Whatever you choose, I'm behind you."

The bar slipped into quiet as both of them got submerged in thoughts. Except for the hum of Teheran-ro traffic outside—evening rush in Seoul's unofficial "Silicon Valley," where venture capital streamed beneath corporate billboards—they both could hear their breathing.

Two years earlier, Jin-ho's world had collapsed with the death of his wife, Min-seo.

On the day it happened, lightning slashed across the grey sky, illuminating her frail form crumpled beneath a fallen crane at a construction site run by Mirae Urban Holdings, a company deeply entwined with politicians and hidden power brokers in Gangnam. The crane's arm lay inert across the debris, as sudden and final as his heartbreak.

Within hours, the site was cordoned off by men in suits—lawyers, executives, and officials—making certain frames of the accident. Jin-ho watched from a distance as the men scripted statements behind dark glass, their look utterly unconcerned.

Litigation followed weeks later. Jin-ho attended a single court proceeding in the Seoul District Court, seated behind his court-appointed counsel. Across the aisle sat high-powered lawyers representing Mirae Urban. The unsympathetic lawyers dismissed the event as mere accident.

"She was wearing her raincoat. You said safety protocols were in place," said a teary-eyed Jin-ho.

One of the company lawyers responded with a polished testimony, "We are sorry, sir, accidents happen. It was a downpour and the crane arm was faulty. You don't have to blame anyone because there was no negligence implied."

The company enlisted witnesses who corroborated their story. Maintenance logs conveniently misplaced. The engineer's report was delayed until muddy footprints—evidence of pressure—flattened the integrity of the truth. And by the time the judge gave his verdict, Jin-ho was robbed.

"I find no evidence of criminal negligence. Liability cannot be attributed," the judge said.

There were no charges. No fines. No justice. Just the sterile label of "industrial misfortune."

Rumours circulated that political pressure smothered the case. Mirae Urban's funding channels traced back to tacit support from assembly members, local ward offices, and campaign contributors. One leaked report, from human rights lawyers analysing the case, suggested that officials had mobilized a media blackout, threatening journalists with punitive measures if they revealed too much.

Civic activist groups staged protests outside the court, holding banners that read: 'Who builds Gangnam while citizens die?' But they soon vanished from public view. Event listings expired. Permits were cancelled. Some protest leaders claimed surveillance; others said their offices were visited in the dead of night. The ripple of fear swallowed dissent.

Jin-ho returned home numb, dragging his grief into the night shifts at the bar, through courier runs in Apgujeong, into drawn-out family debt traps. However exasperated he was, he refrained from harsh political statements as his anger might expose him to the same networks that silenced his wife.

His daughter, Soo-ah, became everything to him. She worked harder at Ace Academy so that someone in their family could rise. Her sketches spoke of freedom, light, of futures that might exist beyond this debt-fuelled city. Jin-ho poured every ounce of love and sacrifice into her, determined that the system which killed Min-seo, shielded by corrupt influence, would not destroy his only hope.

In Jin-ho's mind, Gangnam's skyscrapers gleamed not with promise but with cold profit: developers untouched by prosecution, politicians insulated behind layers of immunity. Construction site tragedies vanished from court records. Lives like Min-seo's faded into footnotes of bureaucratic paper.

This injustice settled in his chest like lead. And this was why he would fight to protect Soo-ah and challenge the silence with his own kind of truth.

At home, only echoes remained—her quiet laughter in the kitchen, encouragement when Soo-ah sketched late into the night. Jin-ho vowed then to bear the burden alone. Soo-ah became his anchor. Every shift, every loan, every sleepless hour, he carried for her.

That evening, a crash jolted him back as he was lost in one of his reveries.

The door swung open with reckless force.

"*Jinhoneun eodie issnayo?* Where's Jin-ho?"

A voice growled, low and insistent.

Jin-ho stiffened as Kang-min's enforcers spilled in. Chrome knuckles, clenched jaws, and the hulking figure of Kang-min's men in padded coats and designer jeans stained with arrogance.

One of them smashed a bottle against the counter, glass exploding like gunfire. Jin-ho stepped forward.

"Don't damage the place," he warned, voice steady as smoke.

The enforcer laughed. "Whatever we damage is interest. Boss's interest." He gestured, his hands hauling chairs across the floor.

Jin-ho watched silently as another thug scattered bottles.

"Please, I need more time," Jin-ho said, his face twitching with pain.

"Time's up. Kang-min's time runs short. Next time, we're sending a message that everyone in Gangnam will see."

He looked at Soo-ah, who'd retreated to the shadows, sketchbook clutched like armour. "Worst-case scenario, your daughter. You understand?"

Jin-ho swallowed, voice taut. "Yes."

"Good." The men left, chairs still askew, the bar awash in utter silence.

Soo-ah emerged slowly from the corner with a pale face.

Jin-ho caught her arm. Sweat-slick and shaking. "Soo-ah." He cuddled her in an embrace.

She whispered, voice shivering: "I'm sorry, Appa."

He pressed her sketchbook to his chest. "Don't apologize. I'll fix this."

He turned to survey the wreckage—shards of glass, broken stools—bits of his life cracked and scattered. Outside and above them, Teheran-ro pulsed, foreign tech firms in glass towers, venture capital deals flowing in the light, untouchable, far removed from this bloodied reality.

He knelt, gathering the larger pieces. "Listen," he said softly. "Nothing changes. Soo-ah, this is still your dream. We'll keep moving."

She nodded, tears unwiped. Their world shook with that visitation. But when father and daughter looked at each other, the bond, born of grief and love, was hardened.

She pressed her sketchbook to her chest, trembling. Her father curled her hair back, whispering, reassuring her. The bar's smell of broken oak, stale soju and distant tteokbokki hung heavy in the air.

Jin-ho hesitated before speaking again.

"There's something I need to show you." He led her out into the alley behind Risky Bar, lit only by a flickering neon sign pointing down a dead-end.

Ahead stood the Prince Hotel, an unassuming building hidden on Seolleung-ro 86-gil. At first glance, it looked like a modest business lodging with soundproof windows, discreet entrance, but the locals called it a love motel, a short-stay spot rather than a formal hotel, often offering hourly rooms, minimal interaction, and private entrances, the trademarks of Gangnam's shadowed side.

Jin-ho crouched, cupped Soo-ah's face and looked into her eyes, "We'll stay here tonight to keep an eye on things and be safe."

"What's this place, Appa?"

He heaved a sigh. "Here, rooms are rented by the hour. People come and go. Nobody knows anybody in this place." He held her hands trying to reassure her.

They slipped inside. The lobby was minimal: vending machines, a curtained doorway, and a staff member behind a frosted window. No lobby chairs around. Close by stood the elevator leading to floors whose numbers were programmed on the push-pad panels.

"A love motel? Here in Gangnam?" Soo-ah questioned.

He looked at her wearily. "They're everywhere, Soo-ah. Built in alleys to hide the compromise. The same way developers hide debt using political cover." He paused. "It has protected me from the enforcers once—at least for one night."

Bold slogans painted on boarded windows down the alley spoke of protests: "Stop construction corruption", referring to recent Gangnam scandals implicating major developers and lawmakers.

To passers-by, the Prince Hotel looked unremarkable. But in the night, under city lights that reflected profit above, it became a haven for secrecy, a safe room away from enforcers or prying eyes.

Chapter 2

The Darkness Comes

Beneath the polished panes of the high-rises in Seolleung-ro sat Kang-min, the calculating croupier of chaos, the boss of a brutal loan-shark syndicate with roots wrapped in real estate, political patrons, and roads of deception. He tapped a glass of rye whiskey and surveyed his sleek and dangerous reflections.

Kang-min's past pulsed with poetic perversity—silver-tongued, street-born, and state-shielded. He began in the shadows of Gangnam's concrete corridors, a small-time collector for predatory lenders. With cruelty, cunning, and charisma devoid of conscience, he climbed the ladder. He leveraged chaebol connections and municipal contracts, offering "favours" in exchange for forged permits. Corrupt council members winked as building plans bypassed safety codes. In return, Kang-min financed upcoming campaigns, tucked slush funds into shell companies hidden behind the mirrored facades of the high-rise.

He turned to his lieutenant standing before him. "The municipality funds flows through shell firms, then lands quiet in our accounts," he said with a hint of pride. "Permit delays, safety inspections skipped— chaebol pay the price for speed and profit. And we fund the campaigns. I fix problems."

His lieutenants nodded.

Kang-min continued softly, venom lacing each word, "How much interest on a ₩1 million loan?"

"Two-thousand percent, boss. Within legal ambiguity, and that is if it isn't changed," his lieutenant responded.

Kang-min regarded the city lights, smirking haughtily. "Until someone pushes. But they never do."

Across Gangnam, illegal lenders charged up to 2,100 percent interest. But justice met with so little of them that borrowers sliding into violence became headlines. Just the week before, a group of enforcers led debtors into buses for beatings; four lenders were arrested, caught in flagrante, but people like Kang-min never appear in those reports.

Years ago, news broke of private lenders convicted for charging obscene interest—up to 1,560 percent annually—far beyond the legal 20 percent cap. One syndicate leader received five years in prison. Yet, men like Kang-min always escaped. Their books were buried beneath layers of political immunity and corporate collusion. Poor debtors vanished before subpoenas. What trailed people like him were whispers from journalists about him owning the lobbyists and the lawmaker.

Back at Risky Bar, Jin-ho's hands cradled a worn calendar marked with deadlines. He scrambled savings, pawned tools from night shifts, borrowed from small shops. But the numbers never added up: the usury-driven debt ballooned faster than he could breathe.

A tremor of dread coursed through him every time his phone vibrated. Kang-min's enforcer were checking in, demanding updates.

His total was amounting to ₩500,000 in coins, borrowed. Still not enough. Shaking his head, he mumbled, "One more day. One more day, I shall be free from all this."

His phone vibrated. A pop-up message from an unknown contact: "₩3M due tonight. No excuses."

He shoved his phone away, hands trembling. He ran his hand over the papers. Everything turned bleak in his eyes and mind.

Seconds after midnight, the door crashed open. The red bulb above the door sputtered. Kang-min stood in the red bulb's aura, flanked by three hulking enforcers whose tattooed skins made them look wild and formidable. Jin-ho's heart lurched immediately.

Kang-min, in a voice as smooth as steel, "Jin-ho-ssi." He circled the bar. Bottles rattled, chairs shifted.

Soo-ah stood frozen by Jin-ho's side.

Kang-min, tapping a bottle rim continued, "Payment's past due, and the interest is whooping." He paused to look at Jin-ho with mockery.

Jin-ho, choking back fear, "I—I'm close. Give me one more week."

Kang-min said coolly, "I'll take tonight's earnings then."

Jin-ho swallowed. "It's all I have."

Kang-min tapped a bottle impatiently. It fell and rattled to a wall. "Your debt climbs, Jin-ho. And I can't continue waiting."

He turned and caught Soo-ah with his eyes. With a smirk, he started moving toward her as she cowered beside her father, by the counter.

"Well, in the meantime, I have to take her as collateral to cover cost."

Before Jin-ho could brace himself, a burly enforcer grabbed Soo-ah's arm. Her scream fractured the hush. Another pulled her roughly toward the door; her sketchbook fell, pages fluttering like white flags on mahogany.

"Appa!"

Her cries tore through him. Jin-ho lunged, but the enforcer's fist met him. Bones cracked. His knees buckled. Blood bloomed on his lip.

Kang-min leaned close, voice thinly tender: "She goes with me. She is insurance."

Then they disappeared into the night, pulling Soo-ah through the red-lit streets. Inside, the bar shivered in silence, shards of glass catching the neon from Seolleung-ro.

Staggering upright, Jin-ho cradled Soo-ah's sketchbook, ragged tears mingling with his sweat. He glared at broken wood and overwhelmed whiskey bottles. Each broken plank felt like his shattered ego. He had failed Min-seo, unable to protect her from the construction tragedy. And now, he could not protect his daughter from a monster spawned by debt and corruption. The ache settled heavily in his chest.

He thought of the loans that kept rippling outward, like bruises on his soul. Statistics said Korea's household debt surpassed GDP, the highest of any OECD country. People his age, with children in school, felt shame and desperation from mounting interest that soared as high as 1,560 percent annually. Jin-ho sank beneath numbers far beyond his means, and beneath the powers no one had ever challenged.

When Min-seo died, he always spoke to Soo-ah about catching her light. But now, he felt the glow fading. Each day, interest ate at his savings like acid. Every shift felt like treading water in a storm, him barely keeping afloat. As the debt collectors circled, he realized most debtors in Korea felt similarly alone—63 percent had no one to turn to, and many contemplated suicide.

Now, after Soo-ah was taken, Jin-ho stared at the smeared glass door of Risky Bar, the neon trembling outside. His muscles ached from the beating as much as his pride did from his impotence. He had failed to repay in time. He had failed to shield his daughter. The hush of the bar seemed accusatory—silent glass, empty stools, his own ragged breath. Jin-ho felt he had ceased to exist as a man, as a husband and as a father.

Tonight, though, in his raw humiliation, his sorrow hardened into determination. His failure was shameful. But something else grew in him, a buoying force. He would claw back control, no matter the cost. Because if the system could swallow his hopes so easily, so could his vengeance.

Jin-ho roared, voice hoarse, "Arghhhhhhh! They took you! Nae sesang."

He touched the scattered pages, his world in graphite and ink. He pressed his fingers to broken wood and dropped to his knees. Eyes clenched against humiliation.

He swore then, in broken breath, "I'll kill every interest-moron who stands in my way. I will find you, nae agi, and I'll bring you home. Kang-min, I will burn your empire to the ground." Taking his child had lit a fire in him.

In the polished high-rises above, deals continued. In the streets below, corruption hummed unchallenged. But in that battered bar, with broken furniture and shattered resolve, a battered man burned with rage and rebellion.

Chapter 3

A Call for Help

One night, some days later, Jin-ho sat in the hollowed-out shadow of Risky Bar, gazing the void. He couldn't cry, couldn't scream. He had reached his breaking point, and what remained now was raw, trembling hope. After pondering for a while, he decided for a face-on. He must recover his daughter. But first, he had to reach out to the only four men he could deem as friends: Sun-woo, Dae-jung, Mr. Park, and Detective Lee.

Sun-woo was a wiry mechanic for tools, gadgets and motorcycles. He grew up in Yeoksam-dong, spending after-school hours in mechanics' bays and motorcycle repair shops behind gleaming Seolleung-ro high-rises. As he grew up, he spent his evenings at Menchuru Ramen Bar on Seolleung-ro, a tiny haven with red lanterns and charcoal grills. He'd sit on low stools, cracking bones of menbosha ramen between slurps, steam curling above spicy broth that cut through fatigue. The owners of the shops already knew him by name and his regular option.

There, in Kalamari-kimchi air, he found solace in the banal activities: customers complaining about usury, devs bragging about loans from shadowy lenders, and whispers of debt-collectors cresting corporate waves. When nights grew heavier than engines, Sun-woo ducked into the Prince Hotel. There, he ran his fingers across king-size sheets and sank into warmth. On one such escapade, he'd checked in after midnight. The front desk clerk greeted him at about 1 a.m. in calm English and Korean. The lobby, painted mostly in soft neutrals, glowed faintly under a single ceiling lamp. He lodged in Room 302, soundproofed, with minibar chilled and

TV glowing softly. There too, Hana, an art student from Gangnam Art Centre, met him.

Hana spoke softly, exhaling tiredly. "I needed the break. I drew all day."

She unzipped her hair; steam from the miniature kettle curled in the hush.

Sun-woo said, splayed on the bed, "You needed escape. So did I."

She leaned in. The room warmed, her perfume jasmine-floral. Silent laughter drifted between them. Outside the window, Seolleung-ro's hum felt distant.

"This bed feels larger than life." Hana moaned.

Sun-woo drew her closer, smiling. "Because in here, reality is erased," he mumbled.

Their night unfurled in hushed whispers, her silk hair damp from the shower, her fingers entangled in the crisp corners of hotel sheets. Her sketchbook lay untouched at the bedside. The TV flickered on, a distant drama muted by thick curtains. They stayed tangled until dawn's edge, comfort shared beyond debt, beyond fear.

In morning light, Hana gathered her bag. Sun-woo pressed a few crumpled notes into her hand.

She nodded, kissed his cheek, and left.

He lingered in bed a moment, the scent of lavender lingering.

Sun-woo's stays became ritual. After a night in the grease-kissed air of his mechanic shop or a meal at Menchuru Ramen Bar, he'd vanish behind the hotel's coded elevator system for an hour or three. There, inside sanitized anonymity, he'd reset.

For Sun-woo, Prince Hotel was more than cheap lodging. It was a liminal zone, far off from view, where the tension of the city was suspended and everyone was anonymous. There, human failures softened in shadowed rooms. At dawn, he would return to greasy overalls and unpaid phone calls, and for a brief interval, believe he'd be a man in control.

One evening, Sun-woo took a walk along Seolleung-ro, its cobblestone sidewalk sloping gently, designed to channel rainwater toward street drains, keeping outer edges dry and safe. These stone pavements were common in newer commercial districts because of their ease of repair and aesthetics. The narrow path was painted green, part of a Gangnam initiative to demarcate pedestrian zones and bike lanes, as well as to symbolize a "greenway" pilot in Seoul's broader drive to widen sidewalks and plant more trees.

As he strolled, he nearly collided with Jin-ho, who was fighting fatigue after late bar shifts. Their eyes met beneath the neon glow of the KMGM building which stood like a silent sentinel across the street.

Jin-ho stared blankly at Sun-woo. "Sun-woo-ssi? Is that you? Didn't expect to see you here."

Sun-woo, forcing a tired smile, said cheerily, "Jin-ho nae chingu. You okay?"

They paused on the green strip. Sun-woo's motorbike jacket still smelled of grease; Jin-ho's jacket smelled faintly of stale soju and wood polish.

"I'm trying, Sun-woo. Just…" he stuttered. "I can't catch a break."

Sun-woo's chest tightened. He watched Jin-ho's shoulders slump, the kind of exhaustion born from defeat.

"I know." He touched Jin-ho's arm. "You're not alone."

They stood on the textured cobblestones. Above them, Seolleung-ro hummed with ambition. They stared into the distance, as if they unconsciously understood each other's worry and what they had to do.

Dae-jung was a street-food stall owner with a tough exterior but a heart tempered by loyalty. Dae-jung started young, apprenticing behind a red-canopy pojangmacha stall in Yeongdong Traditional Market, a vibrant enclave tucked off Gangnam-daero, where tteokbokki bubbled red and hotteok sizzled in sugar-stuffed rounds. He learned that street food wasn't just fuel; it was a frontline of resilience. His parents taught him that every customer, whether tourist or tech worker from Seolleung-ro towers, carried their own shame or ambition, and that a bisected hotteok pancake could be an honest enterprise that offered hope.

He eventually bought his own battered cart at the edge of Yeongdong's night market, selling tteokbokki, odeng, soondae-guk, and his signature black-rice hotteok with meticulous purple grain and molten brown sugar filling. Dae-jung stood beside the flames, graciously sipping soup with struggling delivery drivers, offering gyeranppang to sketching students, or lending his cart's generator to small vendors caught in Gangnam District's recurring crackdowns. He embodied the street-food solidarity amid polished façades.

The Loan Shark of Gangnam District

He operated amid tension. Seoul police often razed unregistered vendors, especially in Gangnam District's maintenance zones, seizing carts and arresting operators who appeared suspicious. Dae-jung's stall faced such threats, but the Korea Street Vendors Confederation once stepped in during a protest near Gangnam Station, arguing for vendors' rights. Dae-jung joined as one who understood that silencing was the greater crime.

When groups planned late-night raids or surveillance, Dae-jung's cart became the neutral ground. His job as a street vendor always kept him informed: the hiss of broth, the chatter over cinnamon-sweet mat-jjang tteokbokki, and the glue of community murmurs supplying facts. Among Gangnam's gloss and political rot, his little corner of Yeongdong market stood persistent, a place where the simplest flavours resisted the most corrupt systems.

One late evening under the neon-halo of Seolleung Station, Dae-jung leaned against his pojangmacha cart in Yeongdong Traditional Market, exhausted but his mind still alert. He'd just finished tucking away eggy tteokbokki strands into his bent aluminium pan, wiping hands on his apron. The narrow alley smelled of chili paste, sweet syrup from hotteok, and simmering broth; garbage stacked in polythene bags lay by the roadside, the air pulsed with the tension of vendors facing City Hall crackdowns, a conflict chronicled by the Korea JoongAng Daily. The local authorities were tearing down stalls, having vendors push back and the city's street life nearing extinction.

Jin-ho was clearing the serving table when Dae-jung burst into Risky Bar. Pushing in the door after closing time, he startled Jin-ho.

Feeling a bit embarrassed, Dae-jung spluttered, "Sorry... thought this was open. I... am I too late?"

Jin-ho looked at him, cautiously. "We're closed, but come in if you need a drink."

Dae-jung ducked through, wiping sweat off his brow. He ordered a barley tea to cool off.

The bar's red bulb flickered. Jin-ho poured tea beside him, while fixing a stare on him.

"You look familiar. Aren't you around the street near Seolleung Station?"

Dae-jung nodded, voice calm, "Yes, I sell tteokbokki, odeng, hotteok… that corner tent over there."

He gestured out the window where vendors clustered under tarpaulin, customers laughing over spicy skewers.

Jin-ho leaned forward, "I've walked by your cart. After class, to pick my Soo-ah over there." He gestured to the corner where Soo-ah sat in shadow, head bent over a sketchbook.

Noticing her, Dae-jung offered a gentle smile.

He went over, his cup of tea in hand.

Playfully, Dae-jung started, "Sketching again, Miss? Is this one on fashion or buildings?"

Soo-ah looked up, smiling. "Buildings."

He tumbled outside, came back in and offered her an odeng skewer with a kind nod.

"For focus fuel. I swear my tteokbokki ups sketch quality."

She snorted softly. He left her drawing intact, distantly honoured.

After that night, Dae-jung began stopping by the back alley more often. He'd deliver gyeranppang—warm egg bread—to the bar when business waned. He saw in Jin-ho's eyes the weight of a father's failure, and in Soo-ah's determination a certain hope for Jin-ho. He became more than a vendor or friend. A present help in time of need.

Mr. Park was a retired mathematics teacher, strategy lover, co-signer and survivor. He always loved to share how he had maneuvered a threatening agent once, earning the respect of most agents. It was this claim that drew him to Jin-ho, who related immediately to the his story.

Mr. Park spent decades teaching mathematics at a public high school near Gangnam, preparing students for university exams and tutoring trigonometry after school. His life was orderly: equations balanced, young minds moulded, and weekends spent grading assignments.

Then one day, he co-signed a modest loan for a family friend out of trust and solidarity. But when his friend couldn't meet with the repayment plan, the debt transferred to Mr. Park. Soon, a loan-shark agent began dropping extortion letters, appearing at his doorstep late at night, and sending threats in letters and documents. The agent leveraged joint-guarantee laws, locally called yeondae bojeung, a common debt trap in Korea, where co-signers become liable.

In Park's case, though the principal was small, the interest mounted at predatory rates, late fees stacking daily. He scraped together some savings, sold his car, borrowed from another channel to repay the creeping debt. Finally, after months of terror, the agent stepped back. Though no violence occurred, Mr. Park still nurtured the trauma of the time, the knock-at-midnight collectors, the paperwork threatening exposure of his private shame. Afterward, Mr. Park retired early, choosing instead to work as a strategist, unraveling the scheme of some of the loan sharks. Combining his discovery with that unfortunate experience, Mr. Park swore to stand against injustice in the city.

Park wandered into Risky Bar one evening, carrying pastries. He paused in the low-lit room, portfolio under arm, seeking solace in tea and dim light. He hesitated at the door, then entered.

Mr. Park was hesitant before he asked, "Excuse me, may I sit? Just tea for my thoughts."

Jin-ho nodded and poured a cup, wiping the counter slowly.

"Any friend of silence is welcome here," he replied.

Park smiled faintly. As thunder echoed over Teheran-ro, the two settled into conversation, Park revealing his fear-born retirement from debt fallout, Jin-ho sharing his struggle to keep his daughter afloat.

"I used to teach mathematics nearby. Had to retire early. I once co-signed a loan."

He hesitated. Jin-ho listened in silence.

"It nearly destroyed me. Monthly punishments in silent envelopes. That lender was relentless. I paid, but the fear remained in me."

Jin-ho related to this epidemic, small debt morphing into big consequences. He shared his own ordeal, the bar, Soo-ah's tuition, the enforcers at his door.

From that night, they met regularly. Mr. Park brought pastries from bakery cafés on Seolleung-ro, shared quiet logic puzzles with Soo-ah, and quietly asked probing questions about lending networks.

His strategic mind helped Jin-ho's discover some hidden truth about the money lenders.

Detective Lee was once a Gangnam police officer known for iron discipline. Jin-ho encountered him one late night, and they had a talk weighed with experience and frustration. Detective Lee had lamented about the injustice people dealt with.

Detective Lee had once worn his precinct badge with pride, patrolling Gangnam's polished corridors and shadowed alleys. He rose through the ranks meticulous, incorruptible, and feared. A sentinel who listened to the city's pulse and parsed its crime scenes with the precision of a surgeon's blade. Yet, despite never being a direct target, he bore witness to the deep wounds inflicted by loan sharks: the muggings under flickering street lamps, harassment calls to people past midnight, and young men hospitalized after brutal collections. He saw fear carved into their faces, desperation squeezed from every student's allowance, their lives circling the drain of usury.

While the legal interest cap sat at 20% per year, stories surfaced of illegal lenders charging 1,200% to 3,000%, illicit layers hidden beneath society's thin veneer of economic progress. Victims disappeared and some resurfaced in hospitals. Many reported fake promises of low interest, recycled threats through messaging apps; some found themselves coerced into fraud.

These cases mounted like storm clouds over Detective Lee's conscience. In dozens of reports, investigations were ruled out and closed over missing pages of evidence. When corruption permeated the precincts, like the notorious Burning Sun scandal, revealing ties between the club bosses and police, Lee felt the institution's honour bending. The frustration shook him.

He'd seen higher-ups quietly dismiss investigations targeting lenders with political connections. He'd witnessed undercover footage seized without charges, and perpetrators gliding free behind polished façades. Each excuse, each closed case, pushed him further away from his oath. And yet the flame inside Lee refused to extinguish.

When he couldn't bear this any longer, he resigned. He didn't scream his protest. He simply folded his badge into his coat pocket and walked out, leaving behind hammering echoes of promises unfulfilled. Haunted, but not broken, he carried the weight of what justice should be into the silent relief of civilian life. In leaving the force, armoured no more in uniform, he became a ghost patrolling injustice from the edge.

The night when Kang-min and his men took Soo-ah, Lee found Jin-ho in the alley behind Risky Bar, Jin-ho drowning in his sorrows. Lee approached quietly.

"Late night, sir."

Jin-ho looked up, startled.

"Yea... just... I have a debt collector. And he's just collected more than his money."

Lee nodded, silent and alert. He knew without being told how much devastating it would be for Jin-ho.

"I'm retired but I know how they operate. Unregistered lenders and violent collectors."

He smelled of stale sweat. He asked about the methods, the times, the faces of Kang-min's enforcers, recording details like a proper detective still on duty.

"If you need any aid, I am here."

Under the low hum of Risky Bar's flickering red bulb, the four, Mr. Park, Sun-woo, Dae-jung, and Jin-ho, leaned in like reluctant geometry on cracked wood. Each man wore tension on their faces, nervous, uncertain, but drawn by something stronger than fear. Then the door to the bar whispered as it opened, and Detective Lee stepped inside, the weight of injustice slowing his movement. Under the sputtering red bulb, he nodded in acknowledgement at all seated around the table. Barrels of stale soju and barley tea rested between them.

Detective Lee opened the conversation in Korean, "Gamsahaeyo gentleman, for honouring my invite. I have tracked patterns in precinct files—collection routes, camera blind spots near Starbucks Reserve on Teheran-ro, shifts in Kang-min's team."

He spread a folded, grease-stained map on the table.

Sun-woo leaned forward, tracing lines. His voice was reflective when he spoke. "If we move through east blindside, we avoid guards and surveillance. I can build tools like locks, diversions, small weapons that we can hide in a cart."

Dae-jung nodded across from him. "We can use mine. It runs midnight near Seolleung Station. I use it to hide tools and for intel drops. I'll be the eyes and shield on the street."

They exchanged looks and nodded in agreement.

Lee said, "We infiltrate the system through street smartness and community trust. They won't suspect the presence of the cart."

Mr. Park chimed in, "I'll schedule guard rotations, calculate interest growth rates, and propose time windows. We need to be more strategic and less emotional."

Jin-ho smiled bitterly at the perfect shape of the plan. Finally, he was getting his due back with those sharks.

The Plan was set straight. Sun-woo and Dae-jung would deliver surveillance tools at midnight near Seolleung Station's exit, using Dae-jung's cart as cover. Mr. Park would coordinate intel delivery including maps, guard rotations, safe routes. Detective Lee would watch precinct lanes, alerting the group when enforcers travelled through camera zones or police patrol cars. Jin-ho was to stay low, forwarding daily business logs to Lee, tracking Kang-min's financial moves through informal channels.

As they folded the map and leaned back, the bar's silence felt charged, their tension bubbling.

Then Jin-ho spoke softly, his voice tinged by bitterness. "They smashed my bar. They took her when I ran out of hope. Soo-ah is gone. But she'll come back. I'll bring her home." He looked away to hide his tears.

Detective Lee stood, authority without badge. "You're not alone anymore."

They folded the map, their breath heavy with determination. Outside, Gangnam's glass towers gleamed just beyond the alley, but inside, beneath chipped wood and fractured neon, the first fragile heartbeat of a rebellion pulsed.

Chapter 4

Underworld Mapping

Risky Bar's flickering red ambient light could not mask the intensity now drawn upon its battered mahogany counter. Detective Lee, clipboard in hand, and Sun-woo, a sketchpad and flashlight at the ready, had begun their first live mission: tracing Kang-min's enforcers to uncover the true extent of his empire.

They started at midnight beneath Seolleung Station, where Dae-jung's cart stood proud amid tail end traffic and streetlamp flicker. Steam curled from the tteokbokki pot, layers of hotteok smoke blending with the city's filtered light. Ordinary customers lined plastic stools. Only a few minutes later, a black sedan eased near. Two men, pristine in suits despite the hour, stepped out into the alley, slipping into one of the nondescript towers.

Dae-jung's cart masked their presence perfectly. As hungry students paused for fish-cake skewers or honey hotteok, Dae-jung offered extra broth, nodded kindly, and whispered updates to Sun-woo.

Sun-woo crouched behind the curb. Through his lens, he watched the men, polished leather shoes, synchronized steps, wrists flashing small watches. Detective Lee hovered near the cart, holding binoculars like a surgeon cradling a scalpel. Dae-jung pretended to refuse a cup of tea, murmuring, "Keep this for after," and passed Lee a note which included camera feeds, patrol schedules, current interest escalation reports.

The raw aroma of street food masked their presence from prying surveillance. When the enforcers disappeared into an anonymous office tower on Yeoksam-dong, the four men hardened their eyes with new knowledge.

They followed pedestrian shadows, their heels clicking on tile, jackets rustling as they passed cracked power lockers near modern façades. They traced the men through each turn and each elevator door they entered.

From his duty as a detective, Lee could recognize a pattern with those buildings. Patrol logs and precinct alerts had showed repeated drops at the same lobby, the same time windows. With every transaction—small slurps and folded bills—they tracked the movements. Lee noted license plates, smartphone flashlight glints, and precisely which elevator bank in the Nonhyeon-dong high-rise the men entered.

The office suit towers masked a secret inside: illegal poker tables, baccarat sessions inside high-rise condos, and undercover gambling disguised as private clubs—hold 'em pubs registered as restaurants. Police had shut down similar operations in Yeoksam and

Gangnam, uncovering live broadcast streams from Philippine casinos, professional dealers, and rooms that looked like hotel suites inside office buildings. They moved locations every few months to dodge scrutiny.

On a napkin, Sun-woo scrawled a note that read: "They're cautious, but predictable. Rotate guards at shift change. Cameras loop delayed by frames." He snapped photocopies of security shutter numbers and delivered encrypted voice notes to Mr. Park, who later decoded the maintenance schedules into guard-rotation predictions.

Detective Lee nodded and mumbled, "We'll map their vulnerabilities."

Their mapping revealed a pattern: two of Kang-min's men entered a sleek building on Yeoksam-dong. They carried briefcases but emerged hours later, often exiting through a side door near a café.

The group realized the hideout was likely a high-end gambling den, a private suite within a corporate tower. Membership was strictly managed and untraceable, as it was only by referral, evading the casual arrests and scrutiny regular gambling businesses faced. The group discovered weekend VIP invitations circulated via KakaoTalk contacts. Dealers wore suits; players gambled with chips converted off-site, no direct currency exchanged inside. Security was tight, cameras looped, and the building rotated operations every few months. It was way more than a den of loan sharks. It was an empire.

Kang-min was not merely a local loan shark but a manager over illegal gambling circuits, online betting rings, and political partnerships sealing immunity. Expansive operations ran servers overseas, gambling via apps and Telegram groups, earning billions in profits by shielding participants behind layered technology and shell offices.

The group watched as a man, tagged in CCTV as "key enforcer", climb elevator 23 to the 7th floor of a glass office building and exit through a private stairwell. They traced the path, entry swipe logs, and security camera timestamps, the initial skeleton of intelligence forming in murky neon-stripe code.

When they gathered back at the bar later, they were ravaged by hunger, their eyes gritty.

Mr. Park, pointing to the mapped data shook his head and said, "This is a network, not a local racket."

"We've seen men in suits going inside, not debt collectors, but empire enforcers," Dae-jung affirmed, peering over the data Mr Park had collected.

"True. Now, we have their vulnerabilities anyway," Sun-woo joined in. "Elevator delays, guard rotations, absent logs. Now, how do we prey on these?"

"We must strip away their secrecy," Detective Lee said, his voice distant.

Sun-woo and Dae-jung trained a gaze at him, obviously expecting him to say more.

Suddenly, Jin-ho tapped the laminated lobby logs. "This is how we find her. This is how we fight."

Silence enveloped them. After some time, they closed the map, deciding to rest for a while.

When they resumed later, they mapped the criminal labyrinth, positioning themselves at its threshold.

Sun-woo, pointing to the screen live-feeding them with movements on those labyrinths, said with a taut voice, "When we move, we move through the blind spots. We'll be ghosts."

Detective Lee replied, "If we target the elevator lobby cameras, stagger deliveries, we can gather evidence and vulnerability sequences."

That same night, they moved again. Under the risk of detection, Sun-woo and Lee approached entry points disguised as delivery workers. Sun-woo carried a portable signal jamming device; Lee maintained shadow covering. With wind-chilled nerves, they placed small RFID trackers near lobby turnstiles and elevator sensors. Sun-woo smashed the chip inside a coffee cup, wrapped in duct tape and tteokbokki grease. Lee noticed masked cameras pointed at street-facing windows; they slipped micro-cameras behind potted flowers to capture entries and exits.

Hours later, subtle alerts pinged on encrypted phones: badge swipes logged at 19:12, elevator rides to the 7th floor at 21:04. One escort appeared wearing Kang-min's distinctive cufflinks. Another maintained radio contact during shift handover. All these movements were aptly recorded, evidences piling up.

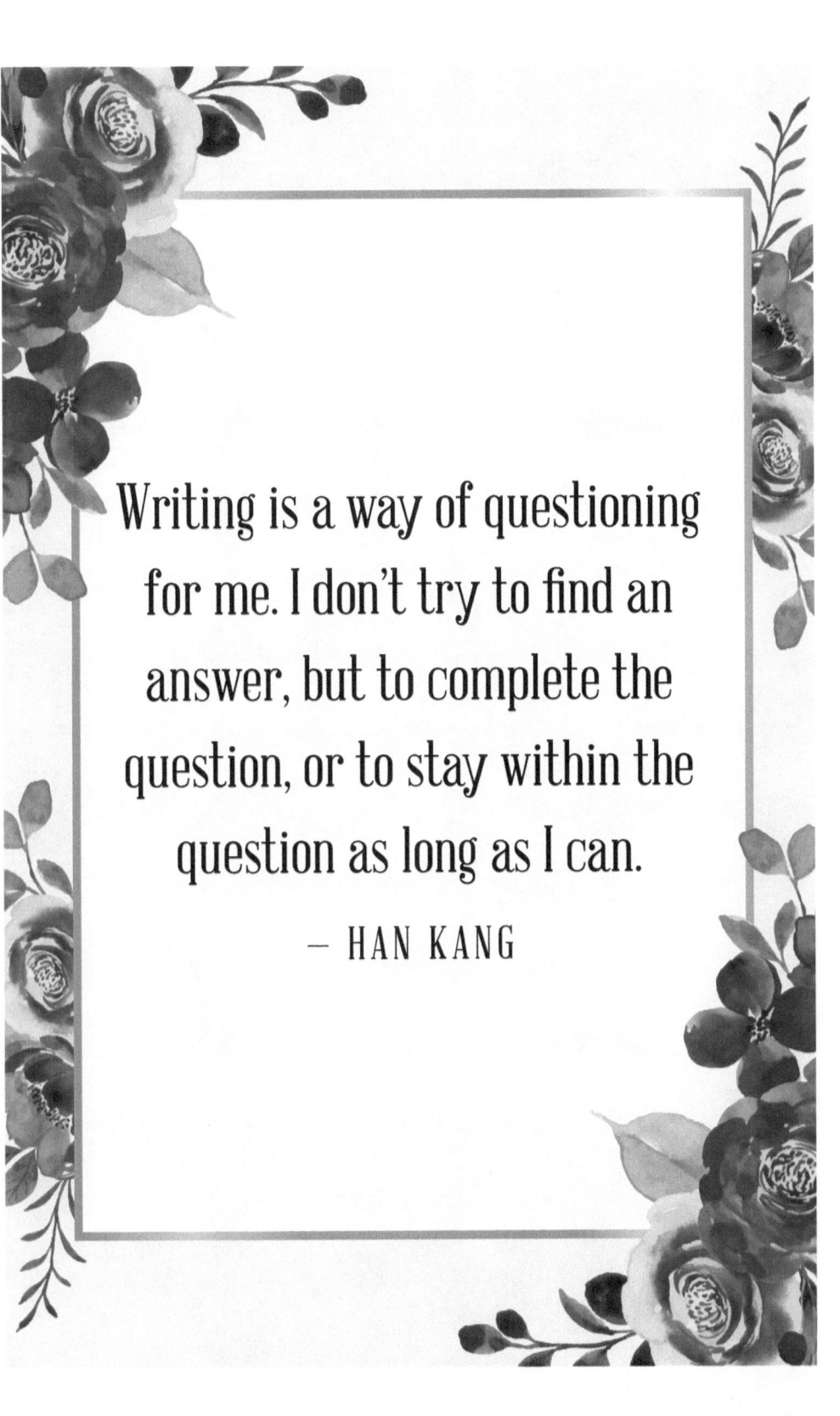

Writing is a way of questioning for me. I don't try to find an answer, but to complete the question, or to stay within the question as long as I can.

— HAN KANG

Book
TWO

Chapter 5

Tools of the Fight

The early evening in Gangnam carried weary promise. Under garish neon and corporate hush, Jin-ho and his allies readied themselves for war before Kang-min's empire could strike again.

Inside a back-facing office basement at Allerman Tower on Seolleung-ro, Sun-woo worked beneath florescent hum of the city. His hands fashioned makeshift weapons from scrap metal and wood. He shaped bats with hidden spikes, nails driven through rubber grip. He also made smoke bombs: small film canisters filled with powdered charcoal and potassium nitrate, sealed in duct tape, with wick made from frayed shoelaces. He tested one under a table, a muted hiss and backdraft of pale smoke decorating the drafty concrete. Across the tower lobby, high-earning office workers passed, unaware of the humble rebellion being born beneath their polished glass.

The next evening, just outside the GS25 convenience store on Teheran-ro 104-gil in Yeoksam-dong, one of many GS25 branches that dot Gangnam's start-up-lined streets, Dae-jung practiced cleaver drills under the glow of the store's fluorescent lights. Meat-carton crates clattered beneath cleaver blows. Passers-by slowed curiously, some stepping closer to watch the violent ballet of wood and metal.

The moonlight glinted on his cleaver as he resumed training with renewed purpose. Each chop shattered one more crate into splinters. Each onlooker receded, some in confusion and others with an understanding that this was no random act, but the making of a revolution they were eager to witness.

The next day, the group's training continued in a tidy, minimalist café tucked near Gangnam Station. Detective Lee led the training session on the rooftop terrace, a secretive space designed for creative meetings above the buzz of Teheran-ro's start-up corridor. While passers-by assumed the café interior was reserved for harmless business meetings and exchange, on the terrace the serious business was far more physical.

Bathed in the cool dusk breeze, Lee stood between Sun-woo and Jin-ho, the city skyline beyond them. On one side sat the café's indoor lounge, bright and sleek, oblivious to the training unleashing above. The luxurious and creative meetings area of cafe struck a sharp contrast to the feral training going on.

Detective Lee, in his methodical and solemn manner, began with lock-escape manoeuvres: wrist grabs, elbow pivots, and leveraged escape techniques.

"If he grips your wrist," he said to the group, "pivot at the elbow and twist for leverage."

He demonstrated some slow-motion technique on Jin-ho, elbow flexing, wrist untwisting, joint clicks faint in the evening air. Jin-ho fell into the break. Sun-woo repeated the moves beside him, tense and precise.

Each repeated move reddened their palms. They practiced with themselves. Lee pressed forward on Jin-ho's attack; Jin-ho stumbled at first, but under Lee's firm eye, he corrected himself mid-fall and regained posture.

As body-joints cracked and they became visibly exerted, Lee calmly advised. "Adrenaline doesn't mean strength. Control brings power."

Sun-woo responded, puffing out hot breath. "When they swarm a cart or corner us in the back room, these moves will let me slip away."

Lee nodded, his gaze steady. Above them, the Ferris lights from COEX, office windows in nearby towers, flickered reminders of polished roofs built on hardened ground.

To decompress after practice, they huddled at Jesus Coffee, a calm café tucked off Teheran-ro, its serene silence and latte rings becoming quite comfortable. Afterwards, they stopped over at Waffle University and when Lee's phone vibrated, it was Park laying out guard-rotation possibilities: "Wednesday's shift change is at 22:15; they swap routes at exit 3 of Starbuck's across Tehran-ro."

At Slow Shot, a small café opposite Starbucks on Teheran-ro, Sun-woo handed Lee some battery packs. "These are smoke bombs. We will throw within two seconds of door sensors. The flash of jamming will make them think it's a camera malfunction."

Lee nodded, testing the battery pack's weight. Nearby, Starbucks bustled with tech workers finishing day shifts, oblivious to the tools being passed across the street.

Back at Risky Bar, Jin-ho finished his late night shift and struggled to lift the spike-bat. The weight strained his arms, sweat clung to his temples. He paused, breath ragged. All his thoughts were on Soo-ah colouring in her sketchbook, her trust solid in him. He closed his eyes and imagined her penciled drawings, her quiet pride. Drawing in strength, he swung again. His arms burned. He gripped the handle tighter. He must protect her, he thought. She needed him and he couldn't afford to fail.

All five of them were at the ready. Gangnam's nightscape gleamed beyond them, the start-up towers, cafés and mirrored buildings. The city thrived above them oblivious of their resolution.

Chapter 6

Ambush in the Alley

The pressure in the air was palpable on the streets of Seolleung-ro, where neon signs from Again Whisky and Izakaya Sooda flickered over the street like indifferent witnesses. Below them, ordinary nights went on, cafés like Oozy Coffee, Frank Burger, and The Coffee Bean hummed peacefully.

Inside his polished high-rise hideout, a glossy boardroom far above street life, Kang-min flipped through financial ledgers. The margins were smudged with red ink. Debts that should have been collected were missing. Payments promised weeks ago had vanished into a void. His calm demeanor cracked.

Immediately, he summoned two of his debt collectors, men in crisp suits, into a private office with mirrored walls.

Kang-min in his trademark smooth-as-steel voice growled, "These sums are missing something. What have you been doing?"

He slapped one man across the face, a sharp, deliberate swing of his arm. Again. His palm imprinted on the man's cheek.

"You're supposed to collect, not waste time with customers who can't pay," he said icily.

The other collector flinched beside him. Both men fled the room, jaw tight, their pride wounded. As punishment, they were dispatched to Gangnam that night to recover the missing ₩50 million.

Walking under the storefront lights, the two enforcers entered the alley that threaded past Again Whisky, turned near Oozy Coffee, and passed Frank Burger. The air smelled faintly of burgers and coffee, the hum of conversation drifting from The Coffee Bean across the street.

They stopped beside the pastel glamour of Cafe BomBom and walked toward AS Coffee, oblivious of the cameras above which logged their every step. The traffic sign on Seolleung-ro overhead blinked a warning they never saw.

Then, chaos erupted.

From behind the glowing neon of Menchuru Ramen Bar, Sun-woo lobbed a smoke bomb into the alley. It landed with a click, and almost instantly, a dense grey cloud hissed outward, swirling into the night air and pushing aside the savoury tendrils of tteokbokki steam. The aroma of chilli and fried dough was swallowed by the acrid plume. Visibility was impaled, and the two enforcers were thrown into confusion, stumbling forward into the smoke's oppressive shroud.

The effect was instantaneous: the thick fog disrupted their vision of the way ahead entirely. In that claustrophobic grey, confusion ensued. Their breathing became ragged and laborious, their eyes burning from particulate irritation. The enforcers hesitated, shielding their faces, disoriented, soaked in dusk and danger.

Sun-woo watched from shadowed cover as they shifted, boots skidding on wet pavement. The smoke blanketed their form like a living cloak. He pressed forward, seeing that they had gained advantage in that ensuing confusion.

Dae-jung emerged almost immediately from the choking haze of smoke. His figure cut through the swirling grey like a blade unwinding its truth. The cleaver in his hand, flat-faced and cold, hummed with purpose.

As the first enforcer thrashed blindly, Dae-jung brought the cleaver down in a controlled arc. It landed on the man's hip, his bones crushed beneath the metal. The man let out a strained gasp and collapsed on the pavement. Dae-jung's motion was precise, fury in his swings.

The second enforcer, startled, lunged forward, arms raised in defence. But Dae-jung pivoted, swinging backhand across the man's chest. The cleaver again caught him on his rib, shredding his leather jacket. Following a crack in his rib cage, the man dropped, slowly losing his breath.

Blood pooled beneath both bodies, dark and decisive. Dae-jung stood over them, his cleaver poised and eyes wild with calm intensity. Unsmiling. His breath settled, ragged yet composed. The alley fell silent under neon glow, but the impact of the combat lingered, etched in bone and hush.

Jin-ho emerged from the suffocating swirl of smoke, the spiked bat arcing through the haze like a pointed vow. He struck the second man on the collarbone with precision. The crack was horrific in its specificity, a fatal break indeed.

The Loan Shark of Gangnam District

The man collapsed, crumpled under the neon gleam and shouted in chaos. Jin-ho stood over the man motionless, grim clouding his face.

Detective Lee zipped forward like a predatory shadow to finish off the men. He grabbed one henchman's wrist, twisted at the nerve junction of the elbow, and slammed him onto the unforgiving concrete. A snap of dislocated bone resounding in the street.

At that moment, a city bus roared to a screeching halt beside Oozy Coffee, its brakes protesting in metallic tones against the asphalt. The doors slapped open with urgency, and two more of Kang-min's enforcers, unaware of the brawl, rushed forward. They emerged blinking into chaos, cufflinks glinting under neon that flickered overhead.

Just then, the group split through their ambush choreography. Sun-woo edged left, Dae-jung and Jin-ho moved centre, Lee circled right, each man acting instinctively.

One of Kang-min's men, eyes wide and faltering, took a cautious, trepid step backwards. Dae-jung saw the hesitation and lunged forward. He grabbed the man's arm, and forced him into the central melee.

Barking mockingly and twisting the man's arms, he said, "No back door tonight, huh?"

Caught between escape and obligation, the enforcer flinched. But he was soon pinned by Dae-jung's lethal cleaver. The blade struck firm at the thigh, tearing through his flesh. The man collapsed, shrieking, face contorted in disbelief.

As the other newly arrived enforcer tried to mount resistance, Sun-woo darted forward, smashing the handguns he held out fearfully. He jammed the enforcer's phones, snapped the memory cards, retreiving an evidence for their case. Detective Lee, in flawless motion, caught the man immediately, locked his wrist, twisted his knee inward, then pinned him with a crushing nerve strike. The man crumpled under such brutal force.

Bus passengers, restaurant patrons at Again Whisky, The Coffee Bean, and employees inside Unit Black, stared through windows as the blood bath went on. The echo of defeat from the enforcers rippled through the street.

The fight ended in minutes. Kang-min's men lay wounded, defenceless, their briefcases sprawled with audited lists and missing-account ledgers. Sun-woo retrieved the red-marked contracts as evidences. The group rifled through and ripped copies of missing entries, then taped them in collective protest to a traffic sign on Seolleung-ro before melting into shadows. They did this to draw attention to the empire's nefarious activities.

Back at Risky Bar, the team reconvened, their hands shaking, clothing stained, breaths ragged.

Mr. Park broke the silence, working briskly. "These ledgers trace back to offshore gambling rings. This is structural, Mr. Jin-ho, not just local debt collection."

Dae-jung, rubbing the cleaver's hilt, began to speak to no one in particular. "They came for owed money. They met justice instead."

Sun-woo quipped, "Security cams fed me logs. There's a second collection team next week in Gangnam Station's sub-basement, same transaction loop."

The detective said coldly, "Now they know they're vulnerable. They'll retaliate, but so shall we. Tonight, we showed them they bleed."

From his high-rise hideout, Kang-min glared at the photographs and CCTV stills scattered across his sleek desk. Two of his debt collectors lay incapacitated—bloodied and battered, their expensive suits torn, wristwatches smashed, their dignity shredded. Loan contracts marked in red ink, the same that had gaped in his ledgers, now lay seized in public view: evidence of both payment failure and brutal retaliation.

Kang-min froze as he listened to Detective Lee's tape. He saw the smoke-bombed alley after midnight. He saw them tape the ledgers to the traffic sign on Seolleung-ro, making public what was meant to remain secret.

He couldn't risk this exposure. If those files reached the press or law enforcement, they could link Kang-min's empire to offshore gambling, illegal collection rings, and violent intimidation. With national crackdowns underway, his shadow network was now in real danger.

Kang-min summoned his lieutenants to the boardroom at dawn and addressed them in a flat and cold tone, "They humiliated us. They exposed us. And now, they've broken the silence."

Silence answered him.

He continued in barely a whisper, "They hit back. They know lines we drew in secret... now they've trampled over them."

He leaned forward. "Sweep all branches. Every CCTV, find witnesses, negate evidence. Silence the story before it echoes, but first, get me his daughter."

One lieutenant ventured, "We've blocked surveillance and destroyed the chips. But the crowd was there and words are spreading."

Kang-min's eyes narrowed. His face hardened. "Retribution is what I want. Make it quiet. Recover what's ours plus payback."

He dismissed them sharply.

As they filed out, Kang-min lingered at the window, gazing down at the glittering towers of Gangnam. Tonight, he would regain control or extinguish it entirely.

Chapter 7

Kang-min's Retaliation

At Kang-min's command, a daylight strike was ordered. Collectors, enforcers, and trusted muscle would descend on Risky Bar during open business hours. They would destroy all remaining assets, send a message of control, and reassert Kang-min's dominance in the city.

By dawn, schedules were drawn. Trucks were loaded. Payments for "expenses" and guards were signed off. Dispatch emails pinged out. Kang-min watched as maps of Gangnam Station, Teheran-ro side alleys, and Seolleung-ro storefronts were annotated with times and exit routes.

The Loan Shark of Gangnam District

This was a calculated retribution, a rekindling of fear. Now, Kang-min readied for retaliation. His ledger might be battered, but tonight, he intended to send a message that would echo louder than the public embarrassment he'd earned.

By early afternoon, Kang-min's hit team encircled Risky Bar like predators. One large thug kicked through the front door. The wood shattered, sending splinters flying, and the door slammed back with a thunderous crash. The scent of oak-aged barrels collided with sharp gasoline fumes wafting from leather-clad thugs. At their entrance, patrons froze, the chatter died down instantly, and waiters halted with glasses raised.

Another brute stormed inside and yanked tables over. Chairs toppled. Bottles skidded across crushed wood and glass, smashing beneath booted feet. Neon lamps collapsed, raining shattered glass into the gutter outside.

Jin-ho's world cracked in that instant. Stained menus drifted upward like injured wings, shattered wood scattered like broken promises. Smoke from fallen torches lit at the bar's edge slithered around the room.

The first thug sneered. "Where's the ledger?" He glanced around, as though looking for an opposition. "You owe Kang-min. You owe us, and you must pay now!"

Inside, the air was clotted with chaos. Jalapeño-stained bar tops glowed under fractured light. Smoke curled over the counter in pale grey arcs.

Jin-ho's voice strained as he let out a weak cry, "Where is Soo-ah? Where is my daughter?"

He stumbled backward, reaching instinctively for his spiked bat, breathing hot grief.

Sun-woo, emerging from behind a stool, lunged towards the men. But another thug swung a heavy wrench, slamming into Sun-woo's temple. The sickening thud echoed, and he crumpled, eyes rolling shut.

Inside Risky Bar, tables lay shattered, menus strewn, the windows smeared with crimson and wood chips. Smoke drifted across bar tops still stained by chilli and broth, once lively, now desecrated by aggression.

Someone screeched, "They're destroying everything!"

Sun-woo moaned from the floor. Jin-ho dropped to his knees beside him. The raid was swift and deliberate, and they limped out through the alley behind Menchuru Ramen Bar, Jin-ho holding Sun-woo, hand around his neck. Across the street, onlookers paused to catch a glimpse near Cafe BomBom and at the taxi stand, their faces carved in shock as Kang-min's group vanished into the heated night air, fulfilled that their message had been well-delivered.

The aftermath at the bar lay naked. Tables turned, wood splintered. A half-filled bottle of soju lay shattered on the floor. Blood splash decorated the counter.

Sun-woo's gadgets—wires and tech pieces—lay in the chaos, torn and broken. Jin-ho's voice trembled but rang fierce as they trudged on in the shadows, "They took my daughter, now they destroyed my home. But they didn't break us."

Amid the disarray lay Sun-woo, pale and still, supported by Jin-ho, both collapsing on the floor. His temple bleeding, consciousness hazy, he lay in the centre of the battered bar. The others soon joined them, rushing to them before more damages could be done to their injuries.

Dae-jung knelt at Sun-woo's side, ripping a napkin from his BBQ stand and pressing it against the wound. Detective Lee held a bottle of antiseptic in one hand and contemplated the bleeding crack in Sun-woo's temple. Inside the bar's gaping doorway, broken electronics and weapon scraps scattered as though it were a playfield.

Sun-woo stirred, eyes fluttering open. Jin-ho grasped his hand.

Sun-woo managed a hoarse whisper. "I... thought I was gone."

Jin-ho replied, voice thick with relief, "You're still here. We still have a chance."

"They won't get away with this," Sun-woo gasped in-between breaths.

Dae-jung dabbed antiseptic with shaking precision, murmuring softly, "Stay with us, brother." Mr. Park silently traced surveillance scribbles with trembling fingers, red ink smeared across fold-out maps now tainted by the bar's ruin.

He collected snapped photos of broken furniture, furniture splinters revealing battering load points and likely injury locations, methodical forensic data for police and media.

With new legislation treating violent loan collectives as criminal organizations, Detective Lee reached a contact at the Special Task Force investigating illegal lending, mandated to act on violent private collections. He also forwarded the data Mr. Park had collected to the contact for legal actions.

Jin-ho had recorded an audio of the bar in ruin—howling sirens, background voices, wood creaks—for forensic time stamping.

Dae-jung repurposed a case of soju bottles and napkins to wrap spare medications for Sun-woo, while also visiting nearby shops like Frank Burger and AS Coffee to request packets of ice, water, and help treating burns on splintered floors.

Sun-woo shifted and sat up, trembling. Jin-ho passed him bottled water.

Within hours, the local dailies carried the damage. The headline on The Korea JoongAng Daily ran: "*Gangnam Bar Raided by Unidentified Men: Theories of Private Debt Violence Under Scrutiny.*"

Police briefing and press conferences ensued. A police spokesperson declared investigations into violent collections would escalate; South Korea's Financial Supervisory Service had flagged illegal lenders charging rates above the legal cap of 20%, with convictions in recent months including cases charging up to 1,560%. The national Task Force on Loan Shark Crimes, declared by the President, was said to be reviewing footage tied to the incident.

With the renewed interest of the authorities, Jin-ho and his group had an edge. All they had to do was to provide the links, the contracts and all the ledger sheets, and everything would become credible.

"If we play this right—evidence, witnesses, public sympathy—we shift from fringe justice to inquiry-led exposure," Mr. Park observed. They were gathered amid the broken tables in Risky Bar.

"I love how their attempts to destroy us dragged them to the light eventually," Dae-jung said.

Jin-ho, holding Sun-woo upright, added, "Yes, open them up and leave them naked."

Sun-woo gave a nod, shaky yet determined. Everything he had to say was encapsulated in the nod.

They left the bar that night. Dae-jung herded the group toward the alley's exit. They steered Sun-woo away, supporting him toward the shadowed exit near Menchuru Ramen Bar, through garbage cans stained by late-night Tteokbokki sauce and abandoned chairs. Outside, convenience lights flickered—Unit Black, Cafe BomBom, The Coffee Bean—citizens stared across streets, sipping drinks, some snapping phones. In the distance, police sirens wailed toward the alley, reporters gathered, fascinated by the ruins in Risky Bar.

The men watched from a distance as Risky Bar's neon sign now flickered with uncertainty. Their resolve tightened at this. Now that they had dragged the sharks to the headlines, it was time to strategize.

Chapter 8

The First Raid

Under harsh studio lights and before a nationally televised audience, Kang-min sat poised, his suit immaculately pressed, expression calm, demeanour composed. He looked too polished for the disaster rocking his empire.

The interviewer, a blonde young woman with her voice direct and unwavering, asked, "Mr. Kang-min, your debt collectors were beaten and publicly exposed. Why shouldn't the public believe there's illegal activity behind your empire?"

A second slipped past before Kang-min answered. He tried to maintain a certain level of composure even though he was trembling inside.

"These allegations are baseless. My operations comply fully with legal standards. Losses are the result of unpaid debts, not violence. My debt collectors are trained professionals, and they would never resort to force."

He tapped a ledger displayed before him, as though to reinforce his version of "facts." It was all a facade which the people understood. What he did was to appear unconcerned and unruffled, to give off the impression of being innocent. This worked somehow.

In the absence of formal charges, and with mainstream media coverage cautiously neutral, Kang-min succeeded in stemming the tide. Despite the attack, police had yet to file formal charges. And the media presence he garnered allowed him to cushion public outrage. In the court of optics, he'd held ground, and claimed that what transpired was debt crisis, not criminal activities.

That evening, the group launched their first major strike on Kang-min's hidden underworld. An illegal poker den masquerading as an upscale "hold-em pub" in Yeoksam-dong. Detective Lee took point, steering the team through shadowed corridors and silent stairwells above a nondescript Gangnam café. Thanks to his detective insight, they intercepted guard rotations in real time. Lee had long memorized the activities of those sharks.

From the half-lit contractor offices, the group descended into the main gambling room. Dim light pooled over green-felt tables while crystal chandeliers cast fractured glints on mountains of chips. The room smelled of cigar smoke mixed with bitterness. Here, liquor, regret, and the unmistakable hum of suppressed fortunes blended in pain.

Inside, the world stood for a moment. Chips stacked atop one another, dealers pressed fingertip against a virtual reel. Everything paused immediately the group entered. The calmness of activities broken.

Dae-jung slithered behind a baccarat table, cleaver drawn like an exclamation point in velvet. In a single slash he upturned things, letting them fly in the air, chips rattling, dealers scattering, players diving for cover as high-rollers shrank behind their chips. Gamblers let out startled yelps and skulked in a corner.

Meanwhile, Detective Lee navigated corridor turns, stealing through each corner. He disabled hidden cameras, slipped into faux uniform jackets, and neutralized two primary guards like they were nothing. He locked one guard's wrist then twisting an elbow until the man crumpled. The second dropped under a swift elbow lock, his strength not matching the degree of Lee's fury.

In the nerve centre, Sun-woo crouched beside a disguised tech rack, clutching a homemade jammer built at Allerman Tower. With a quiet click, he disrupted security protocols. Alarms stuttered, CCTV screens looped stills of empty hallways, lights flickered, then winked out. He smiled as he watched digital feeds collapse into confusion as he severed their vision.

Jin-ho advanced through the dim haze, spiked bat raised like a hammered oath. He brought it down onto the chief dealer's chip tray with a crack that echoed. The dealer reeled and screeched. The group didn't mean to kill. They were there to make a statement, to prove that it was high time the oppressed struck and spoke for themselves.

Through the cacophony of shattering scenes, a rear door whispered open, and Kang-min slipped away, melting into the dark. His escort had staged a showdown with the group, giving him enough time to exit through a secret door, leaving his empire in chaos.

The group finished off the dealers and security aids in the room and made for the Manila-coded logbooks. The ledger files stained with offshore signatures, revealing tying threads to hidden gambling partnerships. Detective Lee gathered the spoils: smudged fingerprints on poker chips, distressed IDs, scratched audio files.

"He ghosted through glass doors," he whispered. "The kingpin escapes, but we have left another mark tonight. These!" He gestured towards the papers. "Are enough evidence for us."

Yet Kang-min remained loose—untethered, unarrested. He had not been within their grasp. The group stood among toppled chairs and shredded curtains, triumphant in exposure but somehow, they felt unfulfilled and thwarted. Their first raid had burned the house, but the owner slipped away through smoke and mirrors. There, they resolved to strike again, and this time, they must go sharper, cornering even the ghost of the scorpion himself.

Through the haze of collapsed chairs and the distant echo of rattling chips, the team gathered near Menchuru Ramen Bar. Dae-jung's hand trembled from the tension and purpose of their fight. He steadied himself by flexing his fingers around the blade's handle.

Sun-woo rubbed at the bruise swelling across his shoulder, pain blooming red through his shirt. He winced as he flexed the joint. Yet he managed a wry smile, at least at what he achieved tonight. He'd managed to install their own camera in the building, and as he tapped the device belt at his hip, small screens blinked with looped stills. His triumph was total.

Nearby, Detective Lee scrolled through security photos on Sun-woo's salvaged device. He examined reflections in shards of glass: VIPs in smoky corners, silhouetted deals, half-written bet lists. He murmured with a clinical tone, "The main deal stays in the data." He pored over the screen one time, his eyes roving listlessly.

"Look here," Mr. Park said, tracing fingers down columns. "Node 47 ties to a Singapore shell, which wires to the Philippines host-chips." He peeled through dealer logs—coded lists, shell company names, IP nodes hidden within Manila-style entries. He pointed to contact numbers scrawled next to blackout dates: proof of money flows disguised in global shuffle—paper trails as damning as a confession.

"That's great," Lee said. "We are getting all that we need." He paused suddenly. "One thing remains and that is dealing with Kang-min. We need to put him down before he makes for safety."

Jin-ho ran his palm across the ledger fragments. "He slipped away, but he'll find us next time."

Detective Lee looked at him with pity and nodded. "We hold the cards now, names, threads, network maps. Time to call in leaks, open press channels, and leverage law. If he doesn't come out, we need to lure him out.

When I taste Korean food,
there's this feeling of home,
of familiarity so primordial,
that it reminds me that I am
inexplicably Korean after all.

— JINWOO PARK

Book
THREE

Chapter 9

The Chase Through Gangnam

From the moment she was torn from her father's arms, Soo-ah's world slithered into a haze of dim rooms and whispered threats. Kang-min's men kept her in a cramped, unlit safe house far from the glitter of Gangnam, surrounded by concrete walls that offered nothing but silence. The lights were perpetually on at night, stripping away her privacy. The walls had no windows, and silence was broken only by the soft scrape of metal chains around her ankle and the dull click of lockable bolts.

Daily, she was forced to stand at shabby walls while debt collectors glared and counted off their losses.

"Tell your father he'll pay."

"Or you'll be next."

"No one owes the boss and still shows that kind of arrogance."

"We won't play the next time we visit him."

The words scratched deep, not only into her flesh but into her hope. Sleep came erratically as fear stung her eyes. Nightmares chased her into waking hours, her mother's face in the wreck, Jin-ho's broken cry reverberating in the concrete.

Meals came late, cold tins of rice slid across the concrete floor with more indifference than nourishment. The portions were tiny, just enough to quell the gnawing in her stomach, but never large enough to calm the storm in her head. Each morsel felt like poison, but she had to eat to survive. Soo-ah learned to treasure scraps of hope in the mistreatment and torture. She found solace in the small gestures by her captors, the offering of clean water and a scrap of fresh clothing.

Yet, each mercy arrived alongside punishment. The safe house had no mirror; she saw only flickers of her former self in cracked tile or the dull sheen of plastic cups. Over time, she stopped trying to trace the face she once knew. They taught her silence ruthlessly. A soft whimper drew a slap so sharp it seared memory into her cheek. Tears were punished with humiliation; raised voices erased with bruised palms. The rule was simple: 'to speak only when given a phrase, to repeat only the lines she was taught.' Phones were shoved to her lips and she was forced to recite, line by line: "I am safe. Everything is okay."

The enforced performances became hollow rituals. The captors recorded her tone, pacing, breath, every nuance monitored. If she hesitated in phrasing or changed inflection—even slightly—the pallid overseer beside her would lean close and hiss: "Do it again." She learned to suppress tremor, bury emotion. Her voice became mechanical and robotic.

Her artistic prowess never died. Still, in her mind, she sketched architectural lines—arches, beams, glass facades reflecting sky—memory fragments of her life at Ace Academy of Design. Each mental drawing was a hope: structures built in her imagination that defied the concrete walls imprisoning her.

Soo-ah's plank-thin meals, breathless whispers, and repetitive forced scripts transformed her into a vessel of oppression. Her identity eroded under psychological siege. In the darkness of her captivity, she learned that survival belonged to silence, her voice a ghost in empty rooms. This breakdown was not only personal. It became currency for Kang-min's power play. It was his way of maintaining dominance and instilling fear in Jin-ho.

The first time she broke the script, slipping out something otherwise, fear coursed through Kang-min at the impending exposure. He ordered closer and stricter enforcement of punishment on her. Her trembling, halting voice in that phone clip became a liability—a sign that she might reveal truth, or worse, falter again. He knew that her fractured identity made her unpredictable. If she broke, the carefully imposed script would unravel. That risk transformed fear into urgency.

So he mobilized. Behind mirrored towers and bourbon-scented boardrooms, Kang-min orchestrated the chase to gain control over her story. His men were ordered to crush Jin-ho's crew before they could sew public suspicion into his ledger. The chase through Gangnam's night was not random violence. Now, his concern was not the brutal collection of overdue debt, but a pre-emptive attempt to contain the narrative.

Even after Kang-min himself slipped through the final alley, vindicated by chaos and smoke, the haunt remained. Late evening streetlights draped Gangnam in gold as Kang-min's men, enraged and unrelenting, burst after Jin-ho's group on foot. The chase sliced through narrow alleys and neon-reflected storefronts.

They fled past the glowing façade of Jesus Coffee, its warm light turning into a hall of mirrors as pursuers reflected in every window. Sun-woo, clutching his injured shoulder, ducked behind an exterior table. He fished around in his pocket and tossed a small, smouldering device. It hissed in the alleyway, wrapping the scene in choking grey haze. Quickly, it wrapped the pursuers, as they staggered through the smoke, a ripple of chaos on the street.

They tumbled past the Starbucks opposite Teheran-ro, banners fluttering overhead, then darted toward Waffle University, its tables abandoned mid-waffle bite as diners banged cups in panic. Their footsteps clattered across the cobblestone street. They skirted Menchuru Ramen Bar, steam billowing over the sidewalk as noodles endured the scream of passing boots. The gang's men faltered at slippery sauces and spilled broth.

Meanwhile, as Sun-woo alerted the group of the incoming danger, Dae-jung guided the team through a tight corridor between Oozy Coffee and Frank Burger, pivoting them into a narrow service lane. Graffiti and dim lighting became their ally. He whispered, "Follow me—I'll carve us a path," before guiding them past crowds startled by the echoing footfall.

Detective Lee led the tail end with composed speed. With one final sprint, they turned at Slow Shot alleyway and slipped into a side entrance into shadowed refuge near Unit Black. They burst in, backs against cold concrete, breaths ragged and hearts synced. Across the neon-bathed pavement, Kang-min's men hesitated at the alley's mouth. Their quarry had vanished into the labyrinth of Gangnam.

Chapter 10

Into the Lair

When Soo-ah's voice fluttered through the receiver, her words mechanically rehearsed, monologues looped in phone recordings, her father was utterly reassured. He pried the voice and words, hunting for clues, a breath too long, a hesitation in a syllable, the faint hitch of false calm. But Soo-ah was never allowed an escape from the routine script. Her overseers controlled the reel, clipped emotional shadows before they could reach Jin-ho's ears.

In one of the calls, Jin-ho noticed she lingered too long on the goodbye phrase, three beats instead of two. Another time, her voice cracked when she said the word "safe", a tremor of panic buried beneath a veneer of calm. These micro-hesitations became their code, pale flags in a minefield.

Each playback felt like both connection and betrayal. Jin-ho held the phone to his ear, drinking in her tone, then closing his eyes to quell the tremor in his chest. Her presence offered solace—then heartbreak as he listened to the subtle sounds of strain in the live rhythm. He could feel her pain cloaked beneath the official tone, but he could not rescue her from it.

It was a cruel paradox. The recurring recordings brought relief. At least, she was alive. Yet each iteration also brought torment since he couldn't reach her. It was the gruelling feeling of this loss that filled him with courage as they moved again towards Kang-min's towers.

Under the cover of night, the group turned their eyes toward Kang-min's high-rise nerve centre, an austere concrete monolith of glass and steel housing the empire's heart. Mr. Park initiated a distraction that paved the way for the group by starting a false fire alarm. Within neighbouring offices, the alarms blared unexpectedly causing a melee. The sprinklers hissed to life, and blaring sirens triggered panic. Security guards wrenched open panels, swore apologies into broken speakers, and scrambled through corridors trying to silence non-existent flames. The chaos bloomed across floors, exposing the security grid before anyone could suspect anything.

As the alarms looped through braided intercoms, Detective Lee and Sun-woo slipped through the main lobby on a side shaft. Security personnel were enwrapped in a confusion. The scanners on the door rejected their credentials and lanyards. The distraction fractured Kang-min's coordination. Instead of disciplined defence, there were fragmented foot patrols and isolated camera operators scrambling to reboot screens. Their nervous apologies echoed as smokescreens of inefficiency.

The Loan Shark of Gangnam District

Within the chaos, the team advanced. Panels that should have traced motion now registered false heat signatures, security lights flickered off, cut short by panic. The corridors emptied at just the right time. Sun-woo masked their presence by hacking building management screens, looping false corridor feeds while CCTV registered only emptiness. The alarms, once meant to deter intruders now aided their successful intrusion.

The world turned silent inside Kang-min's headquarters. Jin-ho and Dae-jung moved stealthily in the quiet. They came face to face with a group of guards. In the lobby's half-lit marble glow, Jin-ho swung once and struck a guard's shoulder blade, shattering it under the precise arc of his spiked bat. Before the second guard could react, Dae-jung descended his cleaver on him, its edge sneaking under lobby lighting and across the man's temple.

The polished lobby desk soon lay unguarded. Jin-ho and Dae-jung didn't pause for breath. They stepped through the silence as though inaugurating a new order.

Beyond the lobby, the corridors took on a clinical hush. Executive wood panels and doors arched overhead, leading toward vault-like entrances and glazed meeting rooms with mirrored windows. Vault-like doors—the threshold to Kang-min's command chambers—stood ominously empty, the heart of his power exposed. In that sterile, meticulous space, the silence felt like invitation. Dae-jung and Jin-ho answered without hesitation.

The quiet before them was as strategic as premeditated. They reached the outer offices. Desks neatly dusted, swivel chairs pushed in, conference call screens dark. Even the smell of filtered coffee offered no welcome. It was as if someone had evacuated every corner, stealing away every detail, in panic.

As sirens hummed and alarms clamoured through Kang-min's corridors, the group edged toward exit routes meticulously mapped by Lee.

Elsewhere inside Kang-min's high-rise, Sun-woo crouched beside the server racks in a shadowed hallway, his fingers working against time and tremor. The locked doors loomed behind him, warding off discovery. Yet he calmly wired small improvised charges to strategic junctions. Each one primed to isolate the control room and fortify their escape route. Despite bruised palms and wincing wrist, his work was mechanical and precise.

A monitor blinked alive with CCTV feeds. Through the flickering frame, he glimpsed the faint shine of Kelly-backed laptops and stacks of encrypted logs, priceless digital records within his reach. From within his crouch, he laid open the core of Kang-min's empire. He leaned in, eyes steady under pain, and copied data onto pressed USB drives, each byte a seed of exposure.

He affixed last fuse strips beside critical servers, setting a timer that would glow olive-green when triggered. Even injured, he worked faster, synchronizing explosives with silent exit windows. The server room's low hum felt almost respectful, as if the hardware understood it was about to betray its masters.

Sun-woo zipped cables shut, tucked drives into his belt pouch, and exhaled with some certainty. In the gloom of Kang-min's inner sanctum, he'd infiltrated the private spaces, breaching secured borders. As soon as he heard footsteps receding in the hallway, he straightened and disappeared into the shadow, creating an injurious hole in the empire's digital security. Kang-min's fortress doors would burn with the sort of information Sun-woo had extracted.

They all made their way to the exit through maze-like doorways, slipping past chaos management teams redlining the building. They struck an unaffected appearance, as though Kang-min's world was not about to rock. Outside, human traffic continued past Frank Burger, Izakaya Sooda, and Waffle University. They emerged into back alleys near Menchuru

Ramen Bar, gritty and alive. What they had would grant them vantage, power, and a taste of justice built from their own scars.

Detective Lee leaked the first documents to investigative journalists: encrypted chats from shell companies, photo stills of ledger pages, server logs—a dossier tied to Kang-min's offshore gambling operations. By afternoon, it was already circulating in the news. The headlines announced boldly, *"Gangnam Underworld Exposed: Evidence Links Hold-em Dens to Offshore Gambling Syndicate"*

"High-rise gambling empire disguised in plain sight"

Key reporters from major Korean outlets cited the evidence Jin-ho's team provided. They published details about alleged accounting discrepancies, fake LLCs, and payment system abuse transforming ordinary cafés into clandestine gambling hubs.

CNN-style coverage from Korea JoongAng Daily ran op-eds drawing parallels to past scandals like Burning Sun, where power and grooming culture marred public perception. Discussion boards buzzed on the television. Everybody was wondering when the police would finally pin the lord behind the empire. At police briefings, a spokesperson stated that the investigation had escalated from "violent private collection" to "organization-style money laundering." Kang-min was then officially on watch.

At Risky Bar, Mr. Park gripped annotated printouts, grinning at the results their efforts were yielding across the city. The ledgers and server logs they released were of public interest, and with them, the people would not forgive Kang-min soon.

The group watched the headlines, the tide pushing in their direction. They knew that with legal weight, public leverage, and truly documented proof, they were no longer underground. They had become catalysts in a broader wave, turning their fight into national outrage, and their injuries into evidence.

Chapter 11

Battle in the Basement

Following the press leak, Jin-ho and the team intensified their search for Soo-ah. They swept through every hidden basement and shuttered storefront along Seolleung-ro, posing as bar repair workers to vendors and pop-up booths behind Unit Black, hoping for some information. Street food vendors and café baristas were adamant on not speaking at first. But under covert pressure, a few of them cracked, mentioning that there were basement-level boards lit at odd hours, men in dignified steps entering and leaving. Detective Lee cross-referenced these information with the flight logs, license plate sightings he had on Yeoksam-dong high-rises, and discovered some matching entries in what he had and what the vendors said.

Late one evening, Lee pinpointed a suspicious basement access beneath Kang-min's high-rise, rented under a shell company that was not widely listed in directory services. The access code logs repeated at odd shifts, and maintenance door returns didn't sync with official records. Jin-ho stared at the data feed, his chest tightening. It was disorienting how such place existed beneath the beauty of the tall buildings.

When they descended through that stairwell, whispering cautiously, the basement door stood worn, its code pad flickering. Jin-ho's heartbreak lifted for the first time. This was the place. It was in plain sight, just the perfect place to hide something. There were no special decorations, no dramatics about it. Such a place rarely attracted attention.

They pushed on stealthily, not desiring to break the ritualistic silence in the basement. Soon, they came to a rusted iron door, half-hidden behind stacked crates in the dim corridor. When they creaked it open, Soo-ah was there, pale, trembling, and bound to a crippled chair. Her lips were dry, her eyes shivered with fear and fragile hope. Her wrists, bruised from rope chafing, shook against the coarse wood beneath her. As her father emerged into view, a tiny glow came to her weary face.

Opposite her stood Kang-min's top enforcer—a towering ex–MMA fighter nicknamed "The Korean Colossus"—barricading her rescue. The man resembled Choi Mu-bae, known in MMA circles as "The Heavy Tank of Busan" for his blend of Greco-Roman strength and crippling power. The man looming in the shadows had shoulders broader than most doorframes. His huge frame beneath the faint light felt immovable.

Soo-ah's eyes fluttered as she listened to muffled footsteps. Her heart thudded hard, trapped inside months of silence. She craned her neck and whispered, "Appa?" The single word cracked the room. The enforcer stiffened, and turned his head. Jin-ho froze for a heartbeat, then lunged forward. Soo-ah pressed back in her chair, her fear mingling with a hopeful tremble. She opened her mouth again, but no word came out.

At first contact, the giant's mass crashed into Jin-ho like a freight train, sending the spiked bat flying from his grip and cold terror shivering up his spine. He crashed into the chair frame, breath knocked out, horrified. "The Korean Colossus" stood immovable, and slowly and menacingly advanced towards him.

But desperation sharpened Jin-ho's senses. As the enforcer leaned in, he bent low, seizing the man's ear between his teeth and sinking deep until he tasted blood. With a wrenching yank, he tore away some flesh. The enforcer shrieked, terrifying and raw, releasing Jin-ho as he clutched at his ruined ear.

Jin-ho didn't wait. He jerked the hidden latch on the chair's restraint, ripping the ropes free in one brutal motion. Soo-ah gasped and shoved the rope off her hands. She stared at her father with relief, while quickly scampering away from the chair.

The enforcer, reeling in pain, clutched his ear while Jin-ho slammed his remaining fist into the man's solar plexus, breaking airwaves.

At that moment, alarms shattered the silence, red lights flickering violently. The steel hallways echoed with the wail of detection. Their presence triggered sirens that raced through corridors. The clangor meant reinforcements were pouring in from every direction, even as Jin-ho gathered Soo-ah into his arms. They made their way up the stairwells and through fidelity passageways.

Jin-ho stood over ruined silence, bloodied and trembling, clutching Soo-ah as alarms echoed. In that brutal moment, while he had trampled Kang-min's captivity, the empire still stood and loomed ahead in the corridors beyond.

Chapter 12

The Den in Flames

The corridor was ignited with strobing red alarms. Soo-ah clutched Jin-ho's shirt and whispered, "Appa...", her words mixing with the rushing air. Jin-ho held her tightly, heart pounding. He understood what she must have suffered in detention. But they must make for safety and evade impending detection.

High above them, lights flickered, panic blossomed in every direction. Sun-woo's little operation in the system had triggered a frantic reaction in the building. He also planted canisters of blinding smoke in the building. The canisters raised plumes of smoke swiftly, suffocating all sight. Jin-ho felt the heat press in as he shouldered Soo-ah, Dae-jung guiding his arm. They moved through spirals of smoke and flame, each breath scorched by urgency.

Sun-woo, with deliberate calm from earlier rigging, re-joined the group just as walls began to groan. The explosives he had planted to stave off the enforcers when the team would escape had already crumbled some walls. As they escaped, the team felt the heat sear their backs, embers raining in fragmented arcs. Still, they pressed on, moving through collapse toward reclamation.

Amid the smoke, Dae-jung and the detective faced a surge of Kang-min's reinforcements sent to crush the breach. While it was chaos at the basement, the gambling den above turned into a battlefield. Dae-jung's cleaver swept in tight circles, deflecting the enforcers in swift arcs. One burly enforcer lunged, only to pivot into Lee's elbow strike that snapped his ribs with a brutal force. Nearby, another charged through burning haze, but Dae-jung intercepted, slicing his arm and dropping him into a shattered pillar. The melee crackled with visceral intensity. Blood, sweat and fear mixing like wet ink on torn ledger pages.

As the fire grew, Sun-woo reappeared, guiding Lee and Dae-jung through secondary exits outlined by emergency lights. Smoke alarms wailed a relentless alarm as the explosives kept pushing down walls. The whole building quivered, and completely lost its menacing and imposing state. The team moved like shadows grafted in purpose, each step compressed with urgency. Flames clawed forward. With the floor splintering and the building giving way inch by inch, their footsteps became threatened.

Amid the chaos, Kang-min, who had came by as soon as he received news of the breach, slipped away through a hidden rear exit. An exit made for such occasion. He vanished into corridors as fired engulfed it. Jin-ho spotted him fleeing near the stairwell and lunged forward. But Soo-ah's whimper held him back, as she was in pain, from both the heat of the explosion and from the torture she had endured. The group gave chase only to be chased themselves by encroaching heat and smoke. Kang-min disappeared into night, leaving only echoes and ash in his wake.

Jin-ho hoisted Soo-ah, Dae-jung supported Lee's arm, and Sun-woo led them through a series of mapped exits. They emerged from the basement complex into a service alley near Menchuru Ramen Bar, their breath ragged and hearts pounding. Outside, the roar of fire trucks and flashing lights greeted them, but their victory was now apparent.

In the fire's wake, Kang-min's network lay exposed, his nerve center reduced to molten debris. As sirens filled the air and policemen approached, the group stood united, with Soo-ah safe, the den destroyed, and a once-hidden empire unravelling in flames. They carried Soo-ah away into the night for treatment. But Kang-min's looming presence remained. Jin-ho vowed to keep moving, to reclaim all the dignity Kang-min had taken from him. He knew that the battle was far from being over, with Kang-min out there. There, he resolved to give Kang-min a pursuit, to end it all at once tonight.

Before Jin-ho moved to pursue Kang-min's shadow through the smoke-choked corridors, he needed to make sure Soo-ah was truly safe. He could not risk releasing her into the labyrinth again, where danger lurked behind each flicker of red strobe. So he pulled his eyes away from the door through which Kang-min had escaped and turned to Dae-jung.

"Hold her here," he said, voice trembling yet steady. "Keep her hidden and calm. Do not leave this place, not until I return."

Dae-jung pressed his palm gently to Soo-ah's cheek, gathering her trembling figure close. He turned to Soo-ah and spoke quietly, like a parent coaxing back broken trust, "We're safe now, Soo-ah. We'll stay in the shadows. I'll keep you hidden."

She nodded, tears soaked through her collar. He guided her deeper into a recom-front corner, away from the flicker of strobing alarms. He pulled his shirt around her small frame to shield her from anything that could be worse than what she'd witnessed.

With a nod, Jin-ho pressed inside his coat and retrieved a handful of Nolans—small tactical trackers with locator tags. "I'll activate these once we're clear," he said. "But if you don't hear me, take her and run." He handed the trackers to Dae-jung and marched further into the corridor with Lee trailing behind him.

As they emerged into the flame-lit stairwell, the alarms crescendoed behind Lee and Jin-ho. They were not worried about the guards and enforcers, as the flame must have pushed them back. Jin-ho closed his eyes, inhaled the night's smoke, trying to steady his mind for the fight ahead. His fist tightened around the bat.

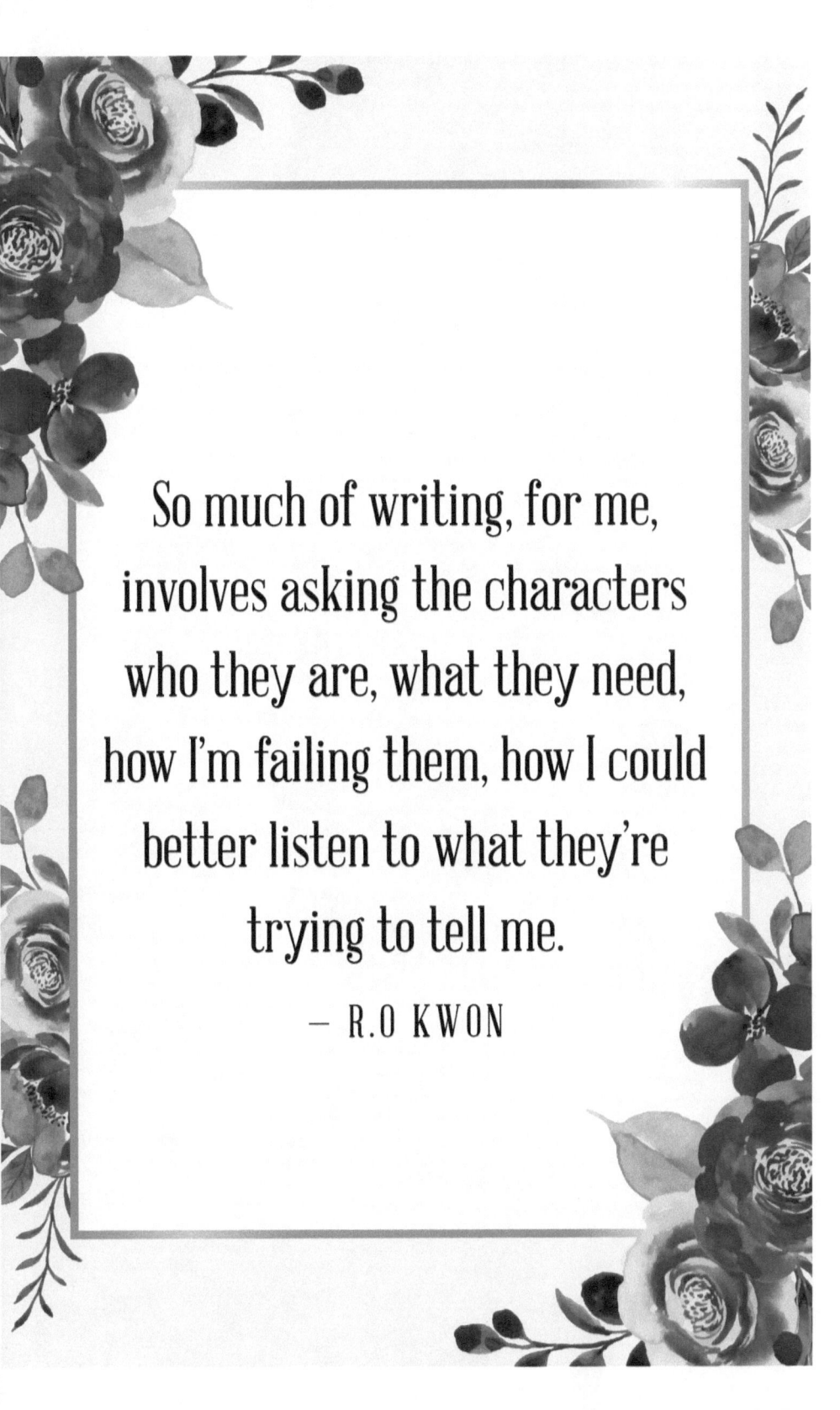

So much of writing, for me, involves asking the characters who they are, what they need, how I'm failing them, how I could better listen to what they're trying to tell me.

— R.O KWON

Book
FOUR

Chapter 13

The Rain-Soaked Alley

The skies over Gangnam opened once they escaped the burning den. Neon glittered on rain-slick asphalt as thick sheets of water cascaded from eaves above Again Whisky and Izakaya Sooda. Water pooled along the green-painted sidewalks, a map of shimmering chaos. But Jin-ho sidestepped the pools. Detective Lee followed close behind, peeling off his coat to his radio and baton plunged to his waist. Neither spoke until a slick, rust-coloured doorway opened into darkness. There, Kang-min stood, still sharp-featured beneath dripping strands of midnight-black hair. The deluge didn't deter him. Rather, it sharpened his focus.

Rain battered the alley walls, turning neon reflections into flickering wounds on the wet asphalt. Jin-ho's shoes skidded, the heavily mossed concrete deterring his approach. But he had seen enough to turn back now. Every drip of the rain on his battered face pushed him further on. The man he pursued stood, holed up in the junction between Waffle University and the service charge entrance behind FFong Grill. The storm's roar swallowed every other sound, save for the waterbeat on metal and Jin-ho's ragged breath.

There, under a gutter overflow and stained floodlight, was Kang-min, arms folded across his broad chest, trousers soaked. He pulled the collar of his once-immaculate suit closed like armour. Rain sluiced into his eyes, but he didn't flinch. It was obvious he had waited for this showdown the whole time.

Kang-min struck first, his palm slicing through the downpour like a live wire, each droplet sensing its charge before impact. Air rasped across Jin-ho's cheek as the strike landed, a blow made slick by water, biting into his flesh with grim intensity. He staggered back. In that moment, the wet ground didn't make it easier for him. His shoes landed in a puddle.

Jin-ho tried to counter the blows that came after, sharp and against his ribs, but the rain betrayed him again. The concrete beneath was quivering with gloss. He lunged, found purchase, then slipped, his arms flailing in the wet wind. Kang-min's boots, however, cut crisp arcs through the water, splashing blooms of liquid with each silent footfall. He pivoted, muscles coiling like steel cables beneath sopping sleeves.

Kang-min spun and thrust forward a kick, aimed at Jin-ho's head. The kick rush heavily towards Jin-ho before he could duck. It landed squarely on his head, and as he landed on the floor, the only sign of life he could register was the cold, wet floor against his flesh. In that blur of motion, Kang-min's years of training showed through every unswerving rotation.

He hadn't climbed to power with just words and money.

But Jin-ho realised that it took him more than strength to be here. It was especially his will to survive that drove him here. Water sluiced into his ears with every breath. The air was wet around him, and the thunder crashed above, swallowing the racing of his heartbeat. His brows stuck to his skin. He puffed out a spray of water, his heart hammering for victory against this shark.

Detective Lee watched from the edge, ready to step in if need be, but even he could see the fight belonged to Jin-ho against the lightning-quick mercenary. Streetlights trembled in the rain-blurred night. The fight was no longer about power. It had become about grit. And in that flash of rain-washed fury, Jin-ho slipped from survival into something like inevitability.

Kang-min's technique rippled with practised precision. Every strike cracked the air with disciplined menace. A spinning uppercut that drifted in like sharp hail, his fist digging into Jin-ho's jawline beneath rain-smothered skin. He threw a reverse hammer-punch, cactus-hard and intended to finish off Jin-ho, moving like scraped metal along muscle. In one seamless motion, he swept Jin-ho's ankle, his knee twisting into neon-laced sludge with a pained crack. That sweep was so mechanical it seemed rehearsed, and Jin-ho's shins slid over slick surface before he collapsed like discarded timber.

The rain above pounded overhead, splattering into jarred ribs, baptising the bruises on Jin-ho's body. Under that curtain of rain, the fight became less about technique and more about survival. As Kang-min landed successive wrist-control blows, dislodging Jin-ho's limbs and breaking his stamina, Jin-ho stared down in resilience. He breathed with broken lungs, the pain sharpened his reflexes, as he searched painstakingly for an entry to get back at Kang-min. He planted both feet in the deluge, anchoring his ankles, energized by the need to keep Soo-ah safe. Her whisper "Appa!" echoed in his ears. He inhaled ice water against cracked ribs. Bones shattered in shock with the blend of grief and fear, but Jin-ho stayed centred.

Kang-min moved fluidly, trading raw force for bone-breaking torque. When he honed in, Jin-ho bent forward with all his fury, pivoted on his heel, and lifted a sponge-tight elbow into Kang-min's collarbone. The strike landed at a textbook downward angle, engineered to crush his bones, precisely what kata patterns and Krav Maga drills guard against. He gripped Kang-min's thigh, drawing hard and digging his fingers in. Before the other could react, he wrenched, drawing flesh and cartilage in the process. That utterly broke the enforcer.

Hovering on the edge, Detective Lee clenched his radio and baton, ready to intercept if Kang-min countered. But Jin-ho was the only one throwing punches now. It was his time and he wasn't hesitant in collecting his due.

Kang-min's eyes wobbled like neon in puddle ripples. All his years of training in the world seemed to have crumpled against that blow of cosmic discipline. He staggered, shoulders sagging under storm and defeat. Jin-ho exhaled through ruptured breath, soaked and shuddering. Kang-min pushed forward again and planted his feet hard on the wet ground, before launching a high kick aimed precisely at Jin-ho's temple. It grazed his wet skin. Jin-ho's sight blurred, heartbeat pounding in sync with a brutal purpose. He must preserve his life if he must mete out a revenge. He dove beneath the arc of the strike, rain-slicked concrete hissing under him. Sliding forward, he tucked low and thrust upward with his knee. The heel of his knee drove deep into Kang-min's abdomen. He further used his elbow, on Kang-min's collar and sternum.

The Loan Shark of Gangnam District

Rain and blood blended on the rain-driven stones. With a jagged, snapping elbow to the jaw, Jin-ho completed the storm-choreographed closing. Kang-min teetered, slowly losing breath, whispered echoes drowned by rain. He collapsed into the gutter, arms splayed and blood pulsing in trailing veins.

Silence followed like a wave breaking. Jin-ho rose, blood dripping from his hair and tie. Detective Lee approached, hands ready on walkie and baton, but said nothing. In the rain-soaked alley, Kang-min's reign died in the thunderous impact of a father who refused to stop.

Chapter 14

Scars and Bonds

Jin-ho and Detective Lee retraced their steps through the narrow, rain-slick stairwell, toward the shared alcove where Dae-jung waited. A single flicker trembled and cast fractured shadows across peeling paint, distorted by puddles pooling at the base of the steps. Outside, the rain drummed steadily against the concrete wall, a relentless rhythm that balanced the hush inside. Soo-ah slumped beside Dae-jung, her chest rising slowly, soaked in the rain. Time seemed suspended between peals of thunder.

Jin-ho moved with deliberate caution, so close that he could feel his daughter's ragged breath and could see the rise of her chest through the soaked fabric of her dress. When he knelt, rainwater slid in cold rivulets down his back, but he barely noticed. He lifted Soo-ah's arm, his eyes fixed on her face. When her glossy eyelashes fluttered open and she focused her eyes on him, he saw how firmly she believed him and had faith in him.

A single tear trailed from Jin-ho's eyes down his to jaw. Soo-ah's lips trembled, then parted a little as she let out a sob. It was a release of the overwhelming emotion bottled over the weeks. In that instant, her past abuse and torture in the hands of the enforcers drowned in her tears. For Jin-ho, the sound of Soo-ah's sob became proof of his triumph, itself the tether that yanked him back from the weeks of guilt-blade doubt.

He straightened, still trembling, careful not to end the sensational moment he was having with his daughter. Soo-ah's breaths slowed and aligned with his heartbeat in a perfect rhythm. Dae-jung rose to steady her, and Detective Lee stepped back to create more room for them. Outside, the storm raged on, water pounding fast. But but down here, in the battered calm of the corridors, Jin-ho and his daughter rekindled their burning bond.

Outside, the crew formed a circle before the ruined entrance of Kang-min's hideout. A haze of smoke curled everywhere—walls still smouldered, their concrete bearing the dark patches of smoke. Water trickled across charred wood and cracked tile.

Their legs trembled; the adrenaline haze hadn't worn off. Clothes were soaked with water and smoke. Dae-jung and Sun-woo locked eyes then exchanged curt nods, both understanding the risk of their effort and the worth of this risk.

Mr. Park straightened his coat, brushed ash from his glasses, and finally broke the quiet. "This is such a glorious night. We will now rebuild. The bar. Our lives. Our hope."

His voice was dry, still fragile from shouting information into smoke-filled rooms. The others nodded, the ruins of the street and the building in front of them.

Detective Lee stood silent clutching his radio. He had spent nights tracing threads of Brotherhood, untangling ledger lies, surveillance lies. Now at the threshold of ruin, amid silhouettes of defeat and defiance, he realised what had kept them breathing. It was their shared wounds, shared names, shared purpose. They subtly entered an emotional pact. The rain pattered on.

Dae-jung leaned against the ash-crusted concrete wall, like a sentinel shaped from midnight steel, his body bearing scars and wounds of sacrifice and loyalty to the team. Nearby, Sun-woo, fingers thickened from burns and exhaustion, carefully tucked a single photo print of scattered ledger logs into his soaked jacket. Mr. Park lifted battered Manila-code files, cradling them as if feeding exacting seeds of accountability into the night. Shards of debris and broken charger bricks lay scattered like monument fragments. The empire lay in fractured ruins behind them. What lay before then was a path devoid of fear, of the fury and rage orchestrated by monstrous lenders.

Jin-ho held Soo-ah once more. Each breath they shared spoke of their bond, soaked in relentlessness and redemption. His ribs, still sore from the fight, pressed softly against her arm. Each scar on his body reminded him of his hesitations, his failure to protect her. But in the way she held him, he knew he was forgiven. Their eyes lit up with promises of a bright future, of rekindled possibilities.

The rain slowly pattered to a stop. Gangnam's glass towers blinked doubtlessly with dusk's dimming light. In contrast, this ruined threshold meant victory for the team. In the brittle aftermath, the scars accrued in the process strengthened their resolve ad validated their effort. These were their true legacy.

Chapter 15

Rebuilding Together

Risky Bar still stood gutted in the heart of Gangnam, its structure shattered and the vibrant spirit with which it was ran bruised. The oak counters that once gleamed, now lay splintered wood and shards of broken bottles. The neon sign flickered from half-lit wires. Morning light seeped into the gutted interior of the bar, washed walls born anew. Jin-ho, hoodie soggy from last night's rain and fight, entered the disarray of the bar. He observed the ruins and said, "We won't stay shut up forever. Let's reopen. This time, slow and safe." With that, he set to work, placing chairs and tables in their appropriate places.

His friends offered help when they came by. Dae-jung carried welded stools made from shattered tables. Mr. Park obtained a renovation permit for the bar. Sun-woo reinstalled the salvaged lights, and soon the bar glowed under the warmth of yellow lights. Together, they swept the charred floorboards and salvaged broken neon tubing. Shattered old bottles were now gathered and poured away.

As the renovation went on, other café owners from Seolleung-ro offered loan of tables, local vendors teed up herbal soy-ful kimchi stew in solidarity. A sympathetic colleague at Restart 119 platform provided information on low-interest SME government assistance programs that could help Jin-ho bounce back into business.

Weeks passed and the venue emerged anew. Oak counters flanked by reclaimed hanging lights, low-hung to spotlight beauty and a culture of resilience which had brought the bar back. A framed sketch of Soo-ah which she drew herself months ago, was placed behind the bar, a centrepiece reaffirming the sentimental nature of the bar, being not just a place of commerce. Patrons now clustered under soft yellow lamps, contributing and commending Jin-ho for his fearlessness.

Meanwhile, Soo-ah, recovering slowly from the trauma, visited the bar one early morning. She was still shaken, as it was in this bar that her pain began. Her fingers traced the mosaic-glass bottles arrayed behind the bar, each one a tiny map of fractured colour, edges of cobalt, emerald, and amber woven together in irregular geometry.

Jin-ho watched her from across the counter, noting the faint quake in her jaw, the slow rise of courage like dawn itself. In that hushed space between them, he saw her gather herself, pulling herself above the devastation of her suffering. She looked up and met his gaze. Time froze between them. The weight of the past weeks heavy and thick in the air.

Finally, she said, softly, almost as if confessing to herself more than to him, "I will try again, Dad, I want it to be normal, again."

"You are normal, my child." Jin-ho held her in his arms. "You can always get back on your feet."

To help her total healing, Jin-ho engaged a group therapy where Soo-ah and others were attended to by a peer-support counsellor who had herself once walked through similar shadows. Soo-ah began attending hesitantly, but eventually, she fully became a part of the sessions. But instead of engaging, she rather sketched on her board: broken doorframes, slanted tables, ghost-shaped reflections in cracked glass. Line by line she gathered shattered fragments and in drawing them, she summoned narrative coherence from the scattered pieces of memory. Things began to make sense for her and in making sense, she found peace.

She soon started redesigning the bar with her art. The drawn lines, oblique perspectives, scattered glass shards that seemed at once dangerous and beautiful appeared on the bar's bare walls. As patrons settled with their morning coffees, they encountered her collaged, conceptual décor: a raw visual journal of trauma gradually transformed into testimony and empowerment.

In this quietly evolving gallery of self-reclamation, each patron saw a moment of rupture and, alongside it, the fragile, fearless architecture of rebuilding. Above the bar, a canopy of festoon lights spanned from building to building, casting warm pools of amber against the gathering dusk, and creating a quiet stage for this reunion under the glimmer of haloed warmth.

Neighbours, café owners, and old regulars stood arm-in-arm beneath festooned arcs, leaning into one another as lanterns and laughter mingled. Mrs. Lim, who ran the pastry car-go café two doors down, raised her glass to Jin-ho and said with a smile, "It's the first time we've seen the door open again in a long time. We wondered if you'd ever be brave enough."

Another neighbour added, "And here it is, Risky Bar back in bloom."

At long folding tables outside the doorway, Jin-ho, Soo-ah, and Dae-jung sat before steaming bowls of vegetable-potluck kimchi stew, its aroma rich with fermented tang and the deep soul of broth and vegetables. The potluck tradition, where guests bring dishes to share, felt deeply right here. Jin-ho ladled rice into bowls with pride and announced, "This recipe, Dae-jung adapted it to be vegetarian-friendly so more people could enjoy without hesitation."

Dae-jung nodded in agreement, "Soo-ah added the gochugaru flakes at the end, let's let her taste it."

Soo-ah, tentatively stirring a spoon, responded as she let her tongue savour the flavour. "It's good. Real good. It tastes like a serious meal."

They all laughed.

Conversation wove through the crowd like a living thread. It was a bubbly air of community and cordiality. With the enforcers gone, the people took a fresh breath, seeking familiar food. Suddenly, Mr. Park stepped forward on an upturned crate, the crowd gathering hushingly. With the string-lights arcing overhead like constellations newly fixed, he spoke directly into the silence with a voice steady yet infused with gratitude, "People, we've fought the good fight, and we've won. Now, we're open and this space lives because of you, because you all refused to let fear hold us down."

The people cheered and applauded. Mrs. Lim wiped a tear. "You gave us back a place we can call home. This is more than gracious."

"Yes," someone affirmed. "We will keep the light bright."

"Our streets are purified."

"No more imprisonment in fear."

And there, beneath the strung light festoons, the door ajar behind them, the neighborhood thrummed with life again.

Again Whisky, Oozy Coffee, Frank Burger—all businesses lit their neon signs in unison as if casting light on unity. The reopening of the bar made it to the news already, the local opinion pieces commending Jin-ho and his daughter for reviving the city.

In the glow of twilight, just outside the bar, the team gathered. Jin-ho rested his arm around Soo-ah's shoulder. Their silence said more than words could articulate. She leaned in, breath steady. Behind them, embers of conflict cooled, neon haze softened. But the scar of their sacrifice would continually remind them of this moment.

Chapter 16

A Quiet Celebration

They were all gathered at a single, long wooden table in the newly rebuilt interior of Risky Bar. The evening was still and easy.

At one end, Mr. Park sat upright in his chair, hands folded loosely in front of him. Across from him, was Jin-ho, mute and gazing at the low, amber-toned floodlights reflecting off Soo-ah's charcoal-and-glass-shard sketches that now softly wrapped the walls.

Soo-ah, perched on a stool, held a small notebook on her lap. The air in the bar was citrusy, with a pinch of leather polish from the restored barstools. The mosaic bottles caught the soft lantern glow, releasing tiny prisms across the scrubbed, varnished floorboards.

Dae-jung leaned forward, elbows on the table, his voice warm in the cosy hush. "I must say, with all that transpired last month, I wouldn't think that this place would look like this, or feel like home again." He wore a sated smile, one that radiated on the faces of the other men.

Jin-ho nodded slowly, eyes drifting to Soo-ah. "Most days I still feel the weight of the past days, when we lived in terror, when the city bled through with enforcers hounding our lives. I think of what we lost." He paused and gestured around him. "But then I look around, and I remember what we held onto."

Soo-ah closed her notebook and offered a small soft smile. "It's interesting how all the things here that I've drawn are not in pieces. Look at them, those broken pieces hung there where I can touch them without flinching from fear. You know what? They represent how much we've borne and how much we fought. They are broken so we can be whole." Her voice cracked a little at the end. Jin-ho reached and lightly placed his hand over hers. She didn't pull back.

"Spoken like a true artist," Dae-jung said with a smile.

Mr. Park drew in a steady breath. "What are now is much stronger than what we were. You know they say that the scar tissue is usually tougher than the skin it replaces." He smirked. "I don't know if that makes sense but I can see that manifesting in us. Through our pain and losses, we've built something stronger."

"Thank you all for not giving up on my father," Soo-ah said, glancing around the table.

Dae-jung nudged Jin-ho, "We should send a few cards to the rising artists who gave us this paint, charcoal, and stew. That'd be good. It will also help in building the community that we need"

Jin-ho smiled. "Already sorted." After a pause, he began again broodingly, "But, you see what I want is to sit out there again, under the festoon lights, and just let people talk about their stories, like we did that first night."

There was a moment of quiet, as though everyone was washed by the memories of the time when the people had dined publicly without fear.

Soo-ah tapped the side of her notebook and held her father's hand. "Don't worry, Appa. It's work in progress. One day, everything will fall back in place. And someday, I'll draw another version of this bar — same shape, same people — but this time without the brokenness in every line."

Jin-ho squeezed her hand. "The line is what holds our story. And the stories and memories are stronger with the lines still there."

She rested her head briefly on his shoulder. Across the table, Dae-jung began to quietly hum a gentle tune, one she once sang in the bar's old karaoke nights, the melody soft as breathing in a quiet room. Without thinking, others began to hum along, verse by verse. The humming tapped into a shared breath between them, creating a kind of music therapy in its simplest form. A quiet chorus born of presence, grounded in community and healing.

Dusk deepened outside. People and movements thinned out on the street. Inside, they were wrapped in the warmth of their company. They didn't need so much words as they already had their memories to relive and relish.

And so, in the bar, they refused to be defined by their wounds but by the inspiring effects of Soo-ah's charcoal sketches. The chorus they hummed resonated and escalated the intensity of the emotions. Jin-ho held his daughter's shoulder, squeezing gently. Dae-jung and Mr. Park smiled brightly at them, delighted in the bond that had been recreated. The flickering lights outside held promises of future joy.

Epilogue

The cabin door opened, and a rush of crisp air spilled into the jet bridge. Jin-ho stepped out, the hum of Incheon International Airport swelling around him. Announcements came in swift and deft Korean, suitcases rattled on the ground, an espresso machine hissed at s corner. He tightened his grip on the trolley, its hand cold against his palm, and moved with the current of passengers toward the glass-walled arrival hall.

Beyond the immigration counters, Seoul stretched in his mind like a layered map. Streets of mirrored towers, alleys steeped in steam and grit, corners where people made and negotiated their fortune. He had not seen the city in years, yet its rhythm still pulsed in his bones. The air smelled faintly of roasted chestnuts from a vendor near the taxi stand, mixing with the metallic tang of concrete after snow.

As he waited for his baggage, the event in Los Angeles lingered in his mind. He imagined Soo-ah on the curb outside LAX, her smile fragile, the warm scent of tteokbokki drifting from a food truck behind her. He remembered the light in her eyes when she spoke of her designs, the pride that swelled in him because she carried both her heritage and her own defiant vision of the future.

Then, he remembered Risky Bar in the street bathed in neon lights, Kang-min's men tearing it apart, the crash of glass, the hiss of smoke bombs in the Seolleung-ro alley. He remembered the bruises, the blood pooling on cold pavement, the ledgers taped in public view. Every risk, every strike, every sleepless night had been a thread in a single, unyielding effort to reclaim his daughter and confront the shadow empire that had swallowed so many lives without consequence.

He had fought for survival and to make sure his promise to his wife, Min-seo, in her hospital bed was kept as long as his breath lasted.

The sliding doors parted, ushering him outside of the arrival hall and into the city. The cold evening wind cut across his face. Seoul's skyline rose in the distance, its lights glittering against the dark. Jin-ho drew a steady breath. The city had changed. But so had he.

He stepped forward, the trolley's wheels clicking over the pavement. He was ready to walk once more into the streets where everything had begun, and where, in some quiet corner, everything they had fought for still endured.